DUKE THE HALLS
A CHRISTMAS PREQUEL NOVELLA TO THE BED ME BOOKS SERIES

The Duke of Kittredge is that rarest of men—a wealthy, tall, and still-unmarried duke. As such, he's perennially at the top of the "Most Eligible Bachelor" list of the *ton*. Yet, he's never gotten close to landing a wife. Young ladies don't seem to like him. Scratch that. They *revile* him. And he's in complete sympathy with their opinion of him.

Because he is, without question, an insufferable clodpole.

But to please his mother, he's promised to attend a Christmas house party where he will meet a dozen possible future duchesses. He will waltz and carol and stand under mistletoe even as he yearns to cloister himself in his library with a blazing fire, a stack of books, and his dog.

So he does what any rational, right-thinking duke would do.

He runs away.

Enter the down-but-never-out **Franny Cranwell**. After what they've both been through, Franny just wants her little brother to have the most glorious Christmas ever. And he will. She'll make sure of it. Even if it means she has to give an adorably grumpy duke lessons in how to woo a wife.

If only the darling duke weren't so handsome and so brooding and so unintentionally funny.

And such a good kisser.

***

Duke the Halls is a Regency romance Christmas novella and a prequel to **The Bed Me Books** series.

***

Content warnings available on the author's website: www.felicityniven.com.

DUKE THE HALLS

Duke the Halls
A prequel Christmas novella

The Bed Me Books

Felicity Niven

BLETHERSKITE BOOKS

Cover Design by James, GoOnWrite.com

*dedicated to the sunshine of my life—
you don't know you are, but you are*

and to intentional neologists

and, of course, to Christmas

CONTENTS

NOTE TO READERS

One of the characters in this novella loves to make up new
words. These neologisms are deliberate. They are not
misspellings or typographical errors.

PROLOGUE

DECEMBER 23, 1817. LONDON.

No, no, no, no. "Stop, stop, stop, stop."

On her fourth *stop*, Kit seemed to realize Franny was talking to him. He got off her, sweat beading on his forehead. The fall of his trousers was half-unbuttoned, and he had pushed her skirts to her waist.

He knelt between her legs, staring at her quim, panting.

"This isn't how this happens." She sat up and pulled her dress down. When her quim disappeared under the red wool and she hugged her knees to her chest, his eyes slowly came up to hers.

"But you said…?" Confusion had replaced savagery.

"I said we should have amorous congress."

He rocked back onto his haunches. "That's what we're doing."

"No, we're not. You were just taking. Have you learned nothing?" Franny scraped her hair off her face with the side of her hand. "If you do this on your wedding night, it'll be a disaster. An utter disaster."

He scowled.

"And I told you I don't exchange intimacy for anything.

Not for money," she said, ticking her fingers. "Not for lodging in London. Not even for the wonderful Christmas you're giving me and my brother."

He grunted. "Then why did you offer to let me fuck you?"

The exasperating man.

"Fine," he said when clearly, in his mind, nothing was *fine*. "You want me to use another word?"

"I'm in this bed with you because I'm attracted to you, you drumpty. Because I'm wanting and needing. And I thought it might be what you needed, too. So we could concentrate your mind on solving your problem. Your courtship problem. Maybe get some of the blood out of your cock and back into your brain in time for Christmas."

Kit wiped his forehead with his shirt sleeve. He'd shed both of his coats somewhere between the front door and his headlong rush up the stairs of his empty house with her over his shoulder, squealing and laughing.

She shook her head. "But don't plunge into me like I'm a vessel for you. I'm here for your bodily pleasure *and* mine. But you were interested only in *that*."

She gestured at his cock and finally let herself take a good look at it.

Zounds. No wonder it occupied his attention. It was thick and long and dark in color, pushing its way out of his fall. A thing of power and strange beauty. Like the man who possessed it.

"Yes," he said, his voice flat and empty.

When she tore her eyes from his cock, he himself was looking down, his chin against his chest.

"Does this make sense to you?" she asked.

He swung himself away and dropped his legs over the edge of the bed and sat slumped, his trousers still undone, his shirt untucked.

She had chided him enough. Maybe too much. If she kept going, neither of them would get what they wanted.

And she knew she wanted *him*.

"I would like to please you," he said at last, his voice hoarse.

"Why?"

He shook his head.

She busied herself, untying the knots of her bootlaces. "Do you want to please me because I'm your teacher and you're a good pupil?"

He scoffed.

"Or are you a selfish pig-widgeon and you think pleasing me will get you what you want?"

"I'm a selfish pig-widgeon."

She waited.

"But I don't want to be." She saw his Adam's apple go up and down. "With you."

Oh. Oh. If things were different, she could smother this darling bufflehead of a man with affection.

Please, God, please. Let some kind, lovely blue blood have the sense to see in him what I see.

She pried off her boots and threw them on the carpet. The thump startled him, and he looked at her.

"What are you doing?"

She winked. "I'm taking off my things. I don't wear clothes to couple with a handsome man." She stretched out her legs and wiggled her stockinged toes against the side of his thigh.

"You're still going to let me— I mean, we're still going to have amorous congress?"

"I still want to. Do you still want to?"

"Yes," he said in that decisive way he had. But then he shook his head. "No. I'll make a shambles of it."

"It would be wonderful if we made a shambles of it

together. A shambles of the bedclothes. A shambles of—oh, I don't know—the front drawing room, if you'd prefer?"

He groaned and collapsed backwards onto the bed. "I'm hopeless."

"No, you're not." She lay down and slid over so she was curled at his side. "I won't let you be."

He sighed.

She whispered, "Did you hear what I said before?"

"Utter disaster."

She playfully hit his chest. "No." She let her hand stay where it was, over his thudding heart. "The part where I let it slip you were handsome."

His far arm came up, and he put his hand on top of hers.

"You did hear it," she crowed and laughed. "I knew you did."

"Franny." He turned on his side, still holding her hand, and fixed his eyes on her. "Will you tell me what to do?"

"Of course, I will. You sweet hubble-bubble."

He stiffened and pulled back a few inches, frowning, indignant. "You're the hubble-bubble."

"Yes. Yes, I am."

Franny couldn't help laughing. And the Christmas miracle was that the Duke of Kittredge laughed right along with her.

ONE

THREE DAYS EARLIER. DECEMBER 20,
1817. KENT.

Kittredge was in a hurry to escape Little Fricking-Green or wherever the hell he was and hadn't taken particular notice of the girl when they had both climbed aboard the stage coach.

She was an ordinary girl, just like any other girl. No doubt on her way somewhere for Christmastide. No reason existed to give her a second look, let alone a second thought.

They were crammed into the only two unoccupied places, corner seats against the side of the carriage and opposite each other. At first, he kept his eyes glued to the window, searching for any sign someone had realized he had absconded. But his luck held and the carriage rolled away from the coaching inn with no one running after it.

When he finally looked away from the window, the girl held a book inches from her eyes, obscuring her face completely. But within a few minutes, a sound erupted from behind the book.

Golden, warm, pure. Joyous. The most remarkable sound he had ever heard. He needed several seconds to recognize it as laughter.

She loosed her remarkable laugh again, and he noted how it invaded her whole being, sweeping down her legs to make her boots dance and stamp while also rolling up her torso so she shook and swayed with her cackles and guffaws.

For the next hour, she turned pages eagerly, punctuating her reading with that glorious laugh. She rarely let the book dip, but when she did, he spied waves of dark brown hair under her bonnet. Quirking, intelligent brows. Large brown eyes, many shades lighter than her hair. A pert, little nose. Pink cheeks. But her mouth stayed hidden behind the book.

It was maddening.

And his curiosity—rarely stirred by a human being, let alone a female—was getting the better of him.

What was she? A young woman, not a girl. Given her worn clothing and scuffed boots, she might be a gentlewoman who had fallen into distressed circumstances. But there was no possibility she was nobility. She was unchaperoned on a stage coach, for one. And there was her laugh. Any young lady of the *ton* would have had that laugh schooled out of her long ago.

And what could she be reading that was at once so amusing and so absorbing? The book was old, the cover stained, the spine faded to illegibility.

Kittredge maneuvered an arm inside his old hunting coat and found his spectacles. No, the blasted things were no help deciphering the title of the volume. He tucked the spectacles away and scratched at the beard he'd grown over the last six weeks.

As he had every autumn since leaving Cambridge, he'd decamped at the beginning of November to the wilds of Hampshire on a hunting trip with Dagenham and Bevel. Of course, most of the days had been spent sipping whisky and reading books in the hunting box when it rained. But one couldn't claim one had to leave London just so one could read in peace. Or at least Dagenham said one couldn't say that, and Kittredge always deferred to Dagenham in terms of what passed for acceptable.

But where was Dagenham when you needed him? Because Kittredge was wondering if he might interrupt the woman's reading and ask the name of the book.

But they had had no introduction.

Was it proper for a man to ask a woman outside the circle of his acquaintance what she was reading whilst aboard a stage coach?

He didn't know.

He had no idea.

He'd never been on a stage coach before.

Riding on a stage coach was not something a duke did.

Unless, of course, the duke was running away from a dozen young ladies lying in wait, armed with mistletoe, ready to force the Duke of Kittredge through the gauntlet known as a Christmas house party in order to find out for themselves if His Grace really was the arsehole everybody said he was.

But this was his Christmas gift to all those unmarried daughters of earls and viscounts. He was escaping before reaching the estate of the Marquess of Merrifield and consequently sparing everyone a great deal of pain and trouble.

Because he had come to the only possible determination a long time ago.

The Duke of Kittredge was, without question, a complete arsehole.

Oh, gobbledygump.

Franny couldn't stop herself from laughing at the jest book she had bought from the odds-and-ends stall. The jokes were so *funny* and would be sure to earn her some smiles from her far-too-serious little brother.

But she must be such a nuisance to the other passengers in the stage coach. Lady LeClere had told Franny often enough that her laughter was vulgar. And the handsome man across from her with the dirty clothes and the scraggly beard was glowering at her, and the woman next to Franny prodded her with every giggle.

Just as her neighbor's sharpened elbow stabbed her ribs for what must be the twelftieth time, a wonderful idea also struck Franny. A not unusual occurrence since magnificent notions smote her all the time.

I'll buy everybody in the coach a Christmas nibble to apologize for my annoying outbursts.

She had thought to purchase biscuits or sweets at the next stop, but it turned out the coaching inn didn't sell those things. What might divide up nicely? She saw a tray of steaming meat pies come out of the kitchen, and her stomach growled.

"Oh, a dozen of those splendazzling pies, please, each wrapped up, please. Oh, please, as quickly as you can. Thank you, that's lovely."

She nipped back to the coach and passed out the pies, first to the coachman and the outside passengers, then to the passengers inside.

"Happy Christmas, everyone!"

"It won't be Christmas for five more days," grumbled her elderly neighbor with the pointy elbows.

"I'll take your pie since you don't want it," a portly man said and reached.

But the woman snatched the packet out of his grasp. "I was just pointing out it wasn't Christmas yet."

The portly man huffed and sat back.

How odd that someone might object to a gift! Still, Franny didn't want anyone vexed when her intention had been to spread cheer.

"Please don't mind me. I adore Christmas so I start early to make it last as long as possible."

The carriage filled with a chorus of *thank-yous* and wax paper crinkling and murmurs of appreciation and the smell of hot, fresh pastry.

Franny grinned and stood from her seat to get her book out from under her. But the coachman must have gobbled his pie quickly because the carriage jolted forward. She would have fallen into the lap of the woman next to her, if not for a grip on her arm.

The grip belonged to the handsome, bearded passenger who had boarded the coach with her at Little Frittenden-Green.

"Thank you," she blurted.

The man nodded.

Oh, oh. He hadn't been angry at her for laughing. Smoldering was just his natural expression. And his blue-gray eyes now made her feel quite warm despite the chilly day. He guided her back down into her seat and only then did he release her.

I can still feel his fingers. Strong. Capable. Commanding. Oh, crispikins, Franny. Fingers can't be commanding.

But his are.

"What was you laughing at, miss?" asked a youth at the opposite end of the carriage around a mouthful of pie.

Franny smiled. "Some very silly jokes."

"Would you read us a few, miss?"

"Oh, doodly-ho! I don't want to bother anyone more than I already have." She laughed until she caught the eyes of the man across from her, and her chuckle petered out as her heart began to pound violently.

"I could do with a few laughs meself," said her neighbor, biting into her pie with suspicion.

The rest of the passengers chimed in with *yeses* and *pleases*.

All except the absolutely deadly man who was dispatching every bit of her scant good sense with his brooding silence and his penetrating stare and those broad shoulders and muscular thighs.

But the thighs were encased in dirty trousers where his shabby coat fell away from his legs. And that unkempt beard. And there was a hunger in his those stormy-sea eyes.

Poor soul.

Well, if she were to oblige everyone by reading aloud, she couldn't very well eat the pie she had kept back for herself. It would go cold, and she didn't really need to eat it, did she? The coach would be in London soon enough, and she would be ensconced with Ren and Mrs. Tumney in a cozy kitchen where she would be stuffed with all kinds of treats from now until Twelfth Night.

The bearded man with the hungry eyes was still holding his meat pie as if he couldn't believe his luck in getting something to eat. She reached out and put her pie in his other hand.

How rum. Beautiful, finely-wrought leather gloves. She hoped a benefactor had taken pity on his cold hands and the poor man hadn't stolen the expensive gloves.

Stolen! That thought was not worthy of you, Francesca.

The man looked at her as if baffled by the appearance of another pie.

"Please do eat up while they're hot. And a happy Christmas to you."

She settled back, smiled into the pages of her book, and began reading aloud.

Two

Her mouth.

Kittredge groaned silently as his cock stiffened in his mud-spattered trousers.

Her mouth was an invitation to sin. Rosy red. A plump lower lip and a cupid's bow on top. And when she smiled, her lips parted and displayed an adorable gap between her two front upper teeth.

His eyes dropped. Nice, round breasts he hadn't noticed earlier. Were her nipples red to match her mouth? In his imagination, they were.

If he were anywhere else besides a moving carriage, he would have long since disappeared. Found privacy behind a locked door and obtained some relief. But he *was* in a carriage and would have to maintain his barely-civilized veneer.

And he came to be grateful he could not flee because he would have missed the unparalleled experience of listening to this woman with the gap-toothed smile and the sensual lips and the widely-spaced dark eyes reading hackneyed quips from what must be an ancient edition of *Joe Miller's Jests*.

He couldn't remember a better afternoon in his life.

And the best bits were when she could not speak because she was so overcome with laughter, so choked with mirth at the foolishness coming in the next line. And even though nobody in the coach could understand the words that erupted around her helpless spasms of merriment, everyone laughed anyway.

Everyone but himself.

The Duke of Kittredge did not laugh. It was well-known he had no sense of humor.

He did eat his pie, however. To refuse it would be the act of a churl and might hurt the laughing woman's feelings. Although he had no earthly idea why he should care about her feelings.

Besides, he was hungry, having last eaten yesterday just before they had left the hunting box and gone their separate ways—Dagenham and Bevel to London in one private post-chaise and himself towards Little Flicking-Green in another. His intestines had been churning over the sure-to-be-catastrophic Christmas house party looming in his future and he had not been able to fathom eating.

But he had escaped that horrible fate, hadn't he? Post-poned it, anyway, since there was no shortage of invitations for an unmarried duke, no matter how much arseholery was attached to him.

For the moment though, he was safe. And ravenous.

He tore the wax paper, lifted the pie, and sank his teeth into it. It was good. Very good. His pie disappeared down his gullet with unseemly haste.

Could he find a similar pie in London tonight? He would not get one at his club. He would be served a chop or a fowl or a joint. How lamentable when what he wanted was another pie. Or three. And to keep listening to the voice and the laugh of this dark-haired Scheherazade in old boots.

But he wouldn't eat the second pie, the one in his other

hand. He'd put it in his pocket for safe-keeping. It belonged to the extraordinary woman seated opposite him.

At the next stop, the matron next to that very same woman started to stand. Kittredge got out of the carriage to help the older woman down, but the pretty Scheherazade followed him and Kittredge had a terrible moment when he thought she, too, was ending her journey.

But she didn't have her book or her reticule with her. She was just making it easier for the other woman to disembark.

A sweet anguish washed through him. Relief mixed with damnably irksome hope.

After assisting the matron down, Kittredge offered his hand to the Scheherazade, and she flashed her gap-toothed smile at him as she took his hand and mounted the step.

A smile.

He couldn't recall a woman, besides his mother, ever smiling at him. Really smiling. Unabashedly, unreservedly, with no fear, no nervous desire to please.

And he had an exemplary view of her arse as she stepped up into the coach. Lovely and ample, proudly straining the gathers of her pelisse.

Kittredge was a man with few weaknesses. But one was for a shapely, generous bottom whose curves filled his large hands. He flexed his fingers at his sides as his cock once again turned into a pulsing length of iron.

Now I can sit beside her if I wish.

But, oddly, it wasn't immediately clear to him if he would prefer to be next to her or across from her so he could continue to look at her.

Next to her. Yes. He'd already sat across from her. Definitely, he would sit next to her. Maybe the side of her perfect arse would accidentally nudge against him. A meaningless contact to her, but a Christmas gift of a caress for him. His chest got a peculiar ache to match the one in his cock.

But then he was punished for his unusual-for-him shilly-shallying. A gentleman in a beaver hat pushed in front of Kittredge with a "Merry Christmas, my good man."

Kittredge got into the carriage after the fellow and was not pleased with the new seating arrangement. Not at all. His Scheherazade was now one place over with the new male passenger next to her and across from Kittredge's empty seat. And she was smiling and speaking to the man.

Fuckity-fuck fuck fuck hell damn.

Kittredge clenched his fists as he sat in his same spot as before. Moments ago he had been teetering on the edge of something he suspected was happiness, but now he wanted to lash out and curse the world, Christmas, and the pompous nobody son-of-a-bitch opposite him.

When Kittredge's blood began to boil, he usually spiraled into a blind rage which consumed him entirely. But not today. For some reason, today, his fury only heightened his awareness of the Scheherazade. And, after a few minutes, he saw her jump a little in her seat, and she stopped chatting to the man next to her although the forward fellow continued to direct jovial remarks towards her.

Was she uncomfortable? Yes, she was. She hadn't resumed reading. Her cheeks were pale. She was biting her beautiful lower lip, and her eyes were glistening with tears.

Kittredge realized he could no longer see one hand of the man across from him.

He looked again at Scheherazade's troubled face and considered the change.

She didn't like something. She was scared—Kittredge had been taught to recognize fear. And she was trying to edge away from the man, but there was nowhere for her to move.

Was the man squeezing her bottom?

Yes, Kittredge decided. The vile man was. Never mind that Kittredge had thought about touching that beautiful bottom himself. He had only *thought* about it. It took a villain to touch a woman that way without permission.

This must stop immediately.

He considered seizing the man and throwing him out of the now rapidly moving coach. But the man might die. As a duke, Kittredge would not be convicted of murder, but a killing would upset the few people in the world he didn't want to upset.

Not that, then.

But he must do something. What would Dagenham do?

Don't think about it. Just do it.

He cleared his throat and leaned forward.

"Dearest," he croaked. The word had never passed his lips before.

She didn't look at him. So he half-stood, bent over, and said it louder. "Dearest."

She looked up at him, trembling.

"Dearest, why don't we change seats so you can have the light from the window? To read?"

"Uh. Yes, thank you. Dearest." She put her hand in his and went around him, brushing against him briefly, and sat in his seat, still holding his hand.

Kittredge glared at the vile man who was suddenly very busy putting his own hands in his pockets.

"Move," Kittredge growled. "So I can sit opposite *my wife.*"

The man shifted over and Kittredge sat down, purposefully taking up as much space on the squabs as he could. Still Scheherazade clutched his hand, their arms stretched across the carriage. He nodded at her and gestured at her book.

"Go on."

Her brow furrowed slightly.

He had been too gruff. Too ducal. Too arsehole. "Please."

After a moment, she released his hand and took up the

book and began reading aloud again, but there was a quaver in her voice and she didn't laugh.

Why did people—men, in particular—have to ruin that which approached perfection? He didn't know the answer despite having done it many times himself. Could he at least take comfort in the knowledge that it hadn't been his fault on this occasion? Yes, but he was still angry that his Scheherazade had been violated. Shaken. Scared.

At the next stop, the vile man got out as quickly as he could, climbing over every other passenger in order to exit on the other side.

She never stopped reading. Over the top of the book, Kittredge saw her raise her brows at him. He raised his brows back. Then one of her eyes shut very slowly and reopened.

Another first in his life. A woman had winked at him!

A wink meant a shared joke. A private, shared joke.

And a wink from her…well, it was special, wasn't it? In a way that a wink from Dagenham would never be.

That wink slithered under his clothing and coated his skin in a glow as his eyes watered. He put a fist to each eye. Damn. How could he be both an arsehole *and* a soft fool? Crying over a wink.

Stop it. The chit probably winks at men all the time.

At last, she lowered the book so he could see her smile. Within a few minutes, she was chortling again.

He leaned his head back and closed his eyes and let her voice and her remarkable laughter seep into his blood and bones. He would never forget this woman's laugh.

Or her wink.

To call her a chit and accuse her of winking at every Tom, Dick, and Harry was just another example of his arseholery. Thank God, he'd only thought it and not said it out loud. And he'd only thought it because—

Goddamnit.

He hated that her wink felt like the greatest intimacy he'd ever experienced with a woman.

And he was not a virgin.

He sighed and opened his eyes and looked out the window. The sky continued to be gray.

If only it would snow.

If only it would snow so much the coach would be forced to stop before reaching London. Because now everyone inside the coach thought he and Scheherazade were husband and wife and they would have to keep up that pretense. And it would be crowded at the coaching inn because of the snow and people traveling for Christmas and there would be only the one room and only one bed for the married couple to share.

He would not take advantage. He would assure her he intended to sleep in a chair, but if she got cold, she might ask him to join her in the bed so they could use their shared body heat to ward off the chill.

He wouldn't scare her. He would move without haste. He would be deliberate and gentle. She would never know the need pent up inside him. He would keep his mouth shut so he couldn't say something offensive. He would just hold her and warm her against his chest and smell her dark hair and her soft skin.

Bah.

Such things only happened in books.

THREE

No snow fell. Just as Kittredge had anticipated, miracles did not come to pass in the real world of 1817 on a muddy road on the way to London.

Far too soon, the coach was caught up in the traffic of the capital and stopping in the yard of the Swan With Two Necks.

He got out first and handed down *his wife*. But then he was trapped helping the other occupants escape the carriage. However, unshackling all the baggage took time, and Kittredge strode over to where she stood, waiting.

He could have made her his sister. But he hadn't. He had made her *his wife*.

It was no accident. He and his mother were in perfect accord on this one point: Kittredge's life would be so much less lonely if he were married. But he had never met a young woman of the *ton* who didn't hate him after meeting him. Who didn't make him hate himself.

Scheherazade was shorter and smaller than he had thought she was. She had seemed to take up so much space in the carriage. And now, in his mind.

"Here." He thrust the pie at her.

She smiled up at him. "Oh, no. It's a little Christmas gift. I meant for you to eat it. I'll have my own dinner soon."

He still held it out. "As will I."

"Oh. Yes, I see. Thank you." She took the pie. "And I must tell you I'm awfully grateful for your assistance with that other matter. I have a terrible tendency to talk too freely to strangers, and unfortunately some men think it's an invitation, and then I'm in trouble, and I was very glad of your help. Your solution was heaps better than mine."

"Which was?"

"I was about to scream *Unhand me, varlet!*" She giggled. "Then jab a hatpin into his leg, next to his bollocks."

He felt his lips twitch at the picture of this little avenging Scheherazade wielding a hatpin.

But he couldn't keep thinking of her as Scheherazade.

"Your name," he demanded.

"My name? It's L—" She gulped. "Franny. And yours?"

"Kit—"

He had started to give her his title. But it had been so enjoyable to hide behind his beard and his ragged, comfortable clothes today. So very liberating not to have been a duke for a few hours.

"Very pleased to make your acquaintance, Kit." She gave him one more view of that seductive gap between her teeth before she scurried away and seized a satchel that had just been taken off the carriage roof.

He fretted while his own small trunk was freed from its lashings, and then he was off behind her, the trunk on his shoulder.

It was dusk in Cheapside. Franny should not be walking alone. He must know she arrived at her destination safely. And what that destination was.

First, she walked west. Then she ducked into an alley, heading north. He almost missed her doing that. The sly minx. At the end of the alley, she broke into a run and went eastward, doubling back.

Oh.

She knew he was following her. He was just another strange man to whom she had spoken too freely. He put his trunk down.

He must let her alone and hope no evil befell her. Damn. If only he had worn a clean pair of trousers and shaved off his beard. And been in his carriage marked with his coat-of-arms. Then she would have let him convey her home.

But if he had been in clean clothes and his own carriage, it would mean he had waited in Little Effing-Green for the arrival of his valet and trunks full of tailcoats and cravats and waistcoats for every conceivable Christmastide occasion including a Christmas Eve ball. He would be at the house party right now, and he wouldn't have been in the stage coach in the first place.

And he would have never heard Franny's laugh.

Therefore, best not to wish for things.

He turned to look for a hack to take him to his club where he would be shown to a room with a crackling fire. He would soak in a hot bath. His hair would be trimmed and his face shaven. He would eat a succulent meal and drink countless glasses of claret. He would read into the night before collapsing into a soft bed piled high with downy pillows and thick blankets.

He wasn't sure why he felt sorry for himself, but he did.

OH GOOD, she had gotten away from her sweet, bearded *husband*. Yes, she could tell he was kind, most people were, but the way he looked at her made her so thringly—a scramble of thrill and tingly—and she couldn't afford an entanglement. Not now. Possibly never again. Entanglements were for women with secure positions in the world, not ones who needed their brother's tuition paid three times a year.

She gave her pie along with a *Happy Christmas* to the first beggar she saw and began wending her way west again, towards Mayfair where Mrs. Tumney now worked as a cook to a duke.

I have taken up a post in London. I just couldn't bear staying on with the new marquess, Mrs. Tumney had written Franny last spring. *Not after how you and his lordship were treated.*

Franny had written back: *Dear, darling, lovely Mrs. Tumney! I hope you didn't uproot yourself on our account. And please remember Laurence is no longer a lord, just as I am no longer a lady. We are merely Ren and Franny now. He is a brilliant, hard-working pupil, and I am a rather insipidious companion. But we love you just as much as ever!*

In October, Mrs. Tumney had written: *All the servants at the London house have been given leave to go home during Christmastide because Their Graces will be away at a house party. Could you and Master Laurence come have Christmas with me here? We would have a grand time, I promise. I will make enormous feasts, and we'll hang greenery all around the kitchen and carol in front of the fire until our voices are gone. It will be as close to old times as I can make it.*

Franny's bravery had eroded with this letter, and she had wept in gratitude. She had been dreading Christmas this year. At Easter and Michaelmas, her brother had stayed alone at school, and she had stayed with Lady LeClere. That was the bargain she had made, after all. She would be Lady LeClere's companion, and Lady LeClere would pay Ren's tuition.

And how lucky that Lady LeClere had said she could spare Franny during the holiday. Her daughters and their families would be visiting, and they had all been invited to take part in the Christmastide entertainments—dinners, balls, musicales—at a lavish house party nearby. Franny must see it would be best for everyone if she made herself scarce?

Yes. Franny wanted to be as far away from *that* house party as possible. Most things she could muddle through cheerfully, but she didn't think she could bear seeing the house and the servants. Not to mention Michael. Too soon. Too painful.

And now Franny was free-as-a-bird in London with four days before Ren arrived so she could put her head together with Mrs. Tumney and plan a cornucopiousity of Christmas surprises for him. The joke book was a good start, but there should be so much more for him.

Her beloved Ren.

She gave a wide berth to the street on which her father had once owned a town house and where she had so many memories of a life vastly different from the one she led now. What good would it do to think on that? Much better to think about Christmas pudding. And holly. And wonderful Mrs. Tumney in an apron, smelling of cinnamon and cloves.

Franny found the duke's elegant white town house, just as Mrs. Tumney had described, with its singular bright-red front door. She went around the back to the servants' entrance off the mews. *Knock-knock-knock* and Franny was enveloped by the warm arms and soft bosom of Mrs. Tumney. Franny's first hug in ages! It felt so good. She hadn't known how much she needed a hug.

But Mrs. Tumney was in a coat, not an apron. And there was a small portmanteau by the door.

"Lady Fran— I mean, Miss Cranwell, how splendid to see you, dear. I'm so glad you've arrived." Tears rolled down Mrs. Tumney's round cheeks. "But, my…my husband has taken ill."

Mrs. Tumney had a husband? She had never mentioned

one before, and Franny had always assumed Mrs. Tumney was unmarried.

"We went our separate ways over some silliness, years ago. But I received a letter this morning from the vicar, and I must catch a mail coach within the hour."

"Oh, Mrs. Tumney!" Franny squeezed her again. "How frightful! Is Mr. Tumney's illness very serious?"

"I'm afraid so. Otherwise, I would never leave you and his lordship, I mean, Master Laurence. I'm only hoping I won't be too late. I need…I need to ask my husband for forgiveness, you see."

"Of course, you must go! And I'm sure anything you've ever done will be forgiven, you're so good. Now, tell me how I can help you." She pulled a handkerchief from her reticule and put it in Mrs. Tumney's hand.

"Oh, thank you, Franny." Mrs. Tumney wiped her eyes. "There's nothing you need do. Look at what a watering pot I've become! And there's so much to say, but I must rush away for the coach."

Franny felt dreadful for Mrs. Tumney, of course, but suddenly she felt dreadful for another reason. She was alone in London with no friends, no shelter, and not much money after her purchases today. She should not have bought the book or the pies. She was always spending impulsively on frivolities that had seemed necessities in the moment. When would she ever learn?

Mrs. Tumney put her arm around Franny and guided her down a passageway off the kitchen. "Let me show you where you'll stay. See how snug it is? And the next room is for your brother. There's plenty of food and coal for your Christmas together. And everyone below stairs knows you're my guests."

Then Mrs. Tumney kissed Franny's cheek, pressed a key into her hand, and was out the door.

Franny sat down at the kitchen table and unwound her

muffler. Well, it wasn't the Christmas she had planned, but it would certainly be an adventure. She must look at it that way. A fantastic adventure. Her and Ren in London, alone. And staying in a duke's house. For Christmas.

Do you suppose a duke might have a library?

Four

Yes. The answer was yes. The duke had a library. An astounding one. In fact, he had books in every room of his house.

Franny would rather have spent Christmas with Mrs. Tumney, but if she couldn't, how heavenly it was to be here with all these books. And in four days, with Ren. She'd still find a way to make a stupendous Christmas for him.

Balancing a pile of books under her chin, Franny stopped in front of a large portrait on the landing. Oh my, this must be His Grace, Mrs. Tumney's employer. Rather dashing. Very serious. Extremely…what was the word? She couldn't think of exactly the right one. It should be some combination of sumptuous and delicious. Scrumptious? Yes. That was it. The duke was scrumptious. What a grand new word she had made for a man whose muscled legs in tight breeches were definitely scrumptious.

Something about those legs? And his eyes were familiar. But she didn't think she'd met the Duke of Kittredge during her one Season before her long engagement. And she'd have no reason to meet a duke now.

She leaned towards the painting.

Drabbit, she couldn't see the details well enough. But there was no money for spectacles for her weak eyes. She'd have to try to save because if she couldn't read aloud, what good would she be to Lady LeClere? It was her skill in doing all the different voices in Lady LeClere's favorite novels that had helped Franny secure the post despite the scandal. That, and Lady LeClere's brusque charity.

But, no, after her earlier scare about affording lodging in London, Franny wasn't going to regret spending money on the jest book and the pies. It was all in the name of Christmas. She'd find a way to afford spectacles soon. It would sort itself out beautifully.

Franny nibbled an apple from the larder and set herself up in a cozy chair in front of the kitchen fire with a wodge of cheese stuffed into a hunk of bread. She flipped open the topmost book in her stack and was soon lost in the wildering world of zoological philosophy.

Her head jerked. She had fallen asleep. She brushed crumbs off her dress as she got up to bank the fire.

Scritch-scritch-scritch at the back door. Had Mrs. Tumney forgotten to tell Franny about a kitchen cat?

She pulled her shawl around her and unlatched the door, but instead of a tabby curling around her legs, a huge dog with a dark face and the most precious, dangling jowls confronted her.

"Who are you, you enormous puppy-thing?"

A pair of muddy paws landed on Franny's shoulders and a rough, wet tongue bathed her face. She staggered back, laughing.

"Oh, so friendly, so furry, so big! Who are you? Yes, who are you? You love of a thing. You beautiful monster."

The dog dropped down and trotted over to the fire and flopped onto the hearthrug. Franny looked out into the mews but could see nothing save rain and puddles. She shivered and closed the door.

Franny turned and addressed her visitor as she brushed at the mud on her shawl. "Oh, you think you belong here, do you?" The dog put her head down. "Are you hungry?" The dog yawned. "Let me get you some water, at the very least." The dog watched Franny fill a bowl from an ewer and bring it over and set it on the floor. The dog sniffed politely and put her head back down. "Not thirsty either, then?" The dog closed her eyes. "None of that. You'll have to go." The dog didn't move. "Oh, criminy."

This giant dog must belong to some nob hereabouts, but Franny couldn't very well go out and start knocking on doors. And Franny couldn't put the poor creature out in the cold. Not just because Franny was soft-hearted. She physically would not be able to put the dog out if the dog did not want to go.

The lovely beast would have to take refuge here, and tomorrow morning, Franny would get some rope and lead her around the square and see if anyone knew her. What other choice did Franny have?

"All right, you can stay." The dog opened one eye. "But I'm off to bed."

As soon as she heard the word *bed*, the dog lunged forward and out of the kitchen and up the stairs. Oh, no, oh, no. The biggest dog in the world was loose in a duke's fancy town house.

When Franny finally found the troublesome hound, she was lying on the largest bed in the world in the most opulent bedchamber Franny had ever seen.

"Get off." Franny used her sternest voice, which, if truth be told, was not stern at all. "Get off now." She added a frown.

She could swear the dog smiled at her. Franny put the lamp down and took hold of both front paws and tugged.

Nothing. Now it felt like the dog was laughing at her. She pulled again with all her might. The dog didn't budge a single inch.

Buggedy.

Franny couldn't leave the dog here. What if the animal thought this luxurious bed with its dark-red velvet draperies and its carved mahogany posts was the equivalent of a necessary?

Franny sat on the bed. She'd stay right here and make sure nothing untoward happened.

The dog rolled over against Franny and put her legs in the air, and Franny scratched her furry stomach. She really shouldn't encourage the sweetheart to stay, but that belly was begging for a rub. And Franny had been wrong. The dog was not a she. The evidence was clear: the dog was a he.

Franny yawned. She'd unlace her boots and lie down for a while. She giggled. Her first time having a kip with a male and what a big, strong, hairy male he was! And so warm which was good because there was no fire up here. She'd just get under the heavy, quilted velvet counterpane. Oh, perhaps she better get the dog under the counterpane, too. She didn't want the poor pup-monster to be cold and see, now, they could nestle together and be so wonderfully, scrumptiously warm.

She threw her arm around the enormous animal. This was going to be the best Christmas ever. She just knew it.

FRANNY. The usual shortening of Frances was Fanny, wasn't it? But Franny suited the gap-toothed grin with the lush lower lip.

Kittredge pushed his plate away and wiped his mouth with his napkin and then ran the back of his knuckles over his smooth jaw. He would not scratch that soft, pretty skin around her mouth with his whiskers now.

Ha! Of course, he wouldn't. He would never see her again. She was lost in the vast multitude known as London.

"Back so soon, Your Grace?"

He looked up into the grin of the Earl of Burchester. Kittredge stood, and the two men bowed to each other.

"Burchester."

The silver-haired earl cuffed him on the shoulder. "Usually you come back from your sojourn to the woods looking a little less cross. But, if anything, you look more glum than usual."

"Glummer. Not more glum." That was young Danforth, shouldering his way past Burchester.

"Shut it, you fastidious philologist." Burchester chuckled, and Danforth scoffed and raised a *digitus impudicus* and headed towards the crowded table at the far end of the dining room.

Burchester turned back to Kittredge. "Would you like to come over to our corner for some early wassail, Your Grace? Lord Dagenham promised he'd join us later once his purse has been emptied at whatever gambling hell he frequents these days."

Of course, Dagenham would have been itching to get to a card table as soon as he was back in London. And also eager to cadge as many drinks as possible.

"No, I wouldn't."

"Direct as always. Never any false excuses. But I can make up my own. You're tired. Your trousers have some Hampshire mud on them. You hate Christmas. Maybe next time?"

"No."

Burchester guffawed and bowed, and Kittredge sat again. It was a long-standing pattern. A joke of some kind, he supposed. Burchester would invite him to join his party of bachelors, and Kittredge would say no, and Burchester would laugh.

And blast, Burchester was right. The cleanest pair of

trousers from his trunk were still none-too-clean. Kittredge would have to send someone to the town house tomorrow to fetch more clothes.

But he had no intention of staying at his own house. It was one thing to fend for himself while in the hunting box, but quite another thing to do so in London. The empty town house would be so cold, and what would he eat?

Besides, he would be alone. Much better to stay here in the club where he would at least see a recognizable face every day. Even if it was Burchester's.

If only he had found out where Franny lived or where she was staying. He might have taken her…where would he have taken her? To a pantomime where he could listen to her laugh for hours. Or to an inn outside of the city where no one would recognize him. To an inn with a room where he could hold her face in his hands and kiss her over and over again until she whimpered and clung to him, dazed with desire.

Strange. He'd never kissed a woman any more than he had to in order to get her to lift her skirts. Why did he think he would enjoy that now?

And could he manage an hour of appropriate behavior while he seduced her? He'd barely scraped by with other women in the past. He'd always inevitably gone silent or said something rude or done something odd. And eventually, despite his title and his what-he-had-been-told-was-a-largish cock and his extravagant gifts of jewelry, there had been slammed doors and recriminations and hurled epithets that years later he could still recall perfectly.

Arsehole. Boor. Clodpole. Arsehole. Lout. Ninnyhammer. Arsehole.

Yes, *arsehole* was far and away the most popular verdict amongst his previous mistresses, the most recent of whom had seized the book he had been reading while lying on his side in her bed and bashed him about the head with it. Apparently, she had been raging at him for the previous quarter of an hour because he had suddenly left off fornicating and picked up the book instead.

But it had been Cuvier's essay on fossils. So much more interesting than the actress who had been underneath him.

Following that assault to his skull, he had successfully sworn off carnal relations. His supposition was as follows: if he did not indulge in coitus, he would eventually be led by his animal urges to pursue a woman in marriage. His cock would force him to overcome his aversion to courtship.

This theory had not yet been borne out, obviously. And now his abstinence had stretched from Lent of 1815 into Advent of 1817. Almost three years.

And if not for the societal and maternal expectations he produce an heir, he suspected he would be able to stay chaste forever. He had an imagination and a hand. What did he need a real woman for?

Because you're miserable, you lonely wretch of an arsehole.

"It's the most important decision you'll ever make," his father had said to him before he had died. "Choosing your duchess."

But how could Ambrose Hugh Charles James Pembroke, Duke of Kittredge, choose a duchess when women couldn't abide him?

He couldn't.

And so, at the age of thirty-one, he was that rarest of objects—a wealthy, tall, very-much-unmarried duke. To the consternation of his mother.

But, despite knowing he was insufferable, he had always thought of himself as a good son. He had told his mother he would attend the Christmas house party with her. No Bevel or Dagenham, warned his mother. No colossus, no rapscallion wastrel.

He had agreed. Perhaps there would be a minor Christmas

miracle, and he'd find the wherewithal to seek the favor of a future wife.

No. Not this Christmas. An hour after his hired post-chaise had left him at the coaching inn where he was to meet his valet in order to be cleaned up for his arrival at the house party, Kittredge had realized he couldn't. He just couldn't. A Christmas house party would be torment. Hideous. Ritualized suffering. He did not have whatever it took to woo a well-bred young lady on this, or any other, Christmas. He would spend the entire house party silent, apart, staring at the floor, trying to avoid ballrooms, sleigh rides, games of Snapdragon, mistletoe, and the countless other things that provoked his arseholery.

One last seat had been available on a stage coach going to London, so he'd scribbled a note for his valet, snatched up his one trunk, and sprinted to catch the coach.

And then he had heard the remarkable laugh.

Franny's laugh.

The shouted toasts at the other end of the club's dining room—the gentlemen were far too hearty, too hale, too happy, just too damn merry, for fuck's sake—broke into Kittredge's wistful memories of that laugh.

The men should drink up and leave. Grant him some peace to dwell on the miracle of Franny's laugh. And her lips. And arse.

But it was Burchester's set: Danforth and Pike and Long-ridge and even Sir Matthew Elliot. They'd be here all night. Especially once Dagenham showed up. And look, Daventry and Drake just came stumbling in, likely straight from Madame Flora's. It was going to be a raucous night downstairs in the club. The only thing that could make it worse would be an appearance by his rakehell-of-a-cousin, Rhys Vaughan.

Maybe Kittredge wouldn't drink any more wine tonight. He'd send the rest of the decanter over to the reprobates in the corner. And maybe he wouldn't stay up reading. Maybe he'd go to bed early and think about Franny.

First, he better write to his mother and calm concerns that anything was amiss. He must make sure she stayed at the house party and didn't come looking for him. Delay the face-to-face fuss.

And tomorrow he'd go round to Dagenham's rooms and see if the viscount had any idea how to track down a young woman in a city of one and a half million.

That meant he'd get to see Bevel. Bevel was barred from the club after the incident with the Duke of Thornwick's pantaloons, but since Kittredge was in London, he could treat himself to seeing Bevel every day over Christmastide.

And Bevel doesn't think I'm an arsehole.

FIVE

Kittredge was woken by a knock.

"Go away," he thundered into the dark room.

A meek voice filtered through the door. "Your Grace, Lord Dagenham insisted."

"No, I insist—" Kittredge heard a scuffle and the door opened, letting in a shaft of light and a stumbling William Dagenham. The night porter for the club stood in the doorway, wringing his hands.

"It's fine," Kittredge told the porter. The man bowed and closed the door as Dagenham swayed back and forth and Kittredge lit the lamp next to the bed.

"Are you drunk?"

"Yes."

"Do you need fare for a hack to get home?"

"I've been home. Bevel's been kidnapped!"

The viscount had a tendency to become histrionic when foxed. Kittredge got out of bed and made Dagenham sit in a chair and talk sense while Kittredge dressed himself.

What Kittredge finally understood was that Dagenham

had gone home and Bevel was melancholy since he had not been invited along, too, so Dagenham had offered to go for a walk in the rain with him. Dagenham and Bevel both had a great affection for London at night and in the wet.

But once they got to the edge of Hyde Park, Dagenham realized Bevel had disappeared. Dagenham searched for Bevel for ages but had to go home to piss because as Kittredge well knew, unlike Bevel, Dagenham couldn't bring himself to piss outside, no matter how drunk he was. But then he remembered Burchester had said earlier Kittredge was staying at the club so he'd come round to let Kittredge know about Bevel.

"Did you remember to piss?" Kittredge did not want Dagenham to disgrace himself in Kittredge's room.

"Yes. Naturally." Dagenham scoffed as if he had never missed the chamber pot while fuddled. "But why are you here? Aren't you supposed to be merrymaking under the mistletoe at the manor of the Marquess of Merrifield? Mmmm?"

"Get in the bed and sleep off your drink. No, take your damn boots off first."

Dagenham struggled with his boots as Kittredge put on his coat. "Where are you going?"

"Only two people in London like me, and I'm not about to let one of them lose the other one."

Flat on the bed, Dagenham raised his head. "You do know he's a dog, right?"

"Shut up. Go to sleep."

"Happy Christmas, Kittredge," Dagenham said into the pillow.

Kittredge walked Hyde Park for hours, but there was no sign of Bevel.

By the break of day, the rain had long-since stopped, and he was exhausted. Dagenham was likely still occupying Kittredge's bed at the club. Of course, Kittredge could get another room there, but his empty town house was closer. He'd sleep for a few hours, don some new clothes, and then resume the search for Bevel.

The door he had ordered to be painted red six years ago so he could remember which house was his. And the key hidden under the railing here. He let himself in. The air in the house was a bit warmer than outside. And it didn't smell musty. Good. He trudged up the stairs.

And then he got into his bedchamber and…could it be? Yes. Bevel was in the middle of the bed, right where he usually slept. And Kittredge was so happy to see his friend, he didn't pay any mind to the odd lump on the far side of the bed.

Bevel turned his head and looked at Kittredge but did not jump up or bark. He must be exhausted, too.

"Oh, Bevel, boy, you gave me such a fright." Kittredge shucked off his boots and lay down on the bed next to the mastiff. "Missed me, eh? How'd you get in? You naughty, naughty boy."

Still stroking Bevel's ears, Kittredge fell asleep.

Mmmph. All night long, her new friend had been such a wonderfully warm, furry source of heat. And now there was a hard, hot thing wrapped around her, pressing on her, holding her, not letting her move, and it felt so scrumptious. Even the paw or something poking at her bottom didn't bother her.

If only she could dream just a little bit more. About the feral man in the stage coach who wanted to know her name and the stern duke in the painting who gave her a meat pie and didn't laugh at her jokes. How peculiar that they were the same person.

Peculiar. But true.

Her eyes flew open to a bit of sunlight peeking around closed drapes.

No.

The man in the portrait was the man on the coach but several years younger. And absent the beard and the dirty clothes.

No.

Impossible.

But if it were possible, it meant the duke was in London because he had gotten off the coach with her. And this was his house. And she was in *his* bed. With a dog.

She lurched to get out of the bed.

Nothing happened.

She tried again, grunting with effort, straining her stomach in an effort to sit up.

She looked down. Two human arms banded around her middle and held her against the hard, warm thing that must be the human body attached to the arms.

She screamed. The arms released her immediately, and she was off the bed in a flash. The body shot off the bed, too, but on the other side, between her and the door. There was no sign of the dog.

The body was tall with mussed brown hair. The body belonged to the duke, of course, wearing the coat of the man on the stage coach. But he was shaven, so he looked more like the duke than the man on the stage coach. But they were the same person. She knew that.

"I'm sorry I screamed, Your Grace. You gave me a fright."

He rubbed his eyes with his fists. "This is the most realistic dream I've ever had."

"It's not a dream."

"Yes, it is. I went to sleep with Bevel and woke up with you." The smallest upward curving of the beautiful lips that had been hidden by his beard. And were those dimples? "With *you*, Franny."

"Yes, you did. But it's still not a dream. Who's Bevel?"

"My dog."

Oh, that explained a whole host of things. She stooped and picked up her boots and grabbed her shawl and started edging her way towards the door.

"You see, Your Grace, I'm a guest, that is, I was going to be a guest of Mrs. Tumney, but her husband, ill, and I'm supposed to be meeting my brother for Christmas, and then the dog and it was raining and cold and the dog scatampered up here and I tried—" She was almost at the door. But the duke-man had moved with her and was next to her. If she could just slide out the door and run down the stairs and get her satchel and then what?

A warm hand on her cheek. Those commanding fingers.

"Franny?"

She looked up. Yes, dimples. And such a straight nose. And those hungry gray-blue eyes.

"I like you," he said.

"Yes, well, thank you, you're very kind—"

The dimples disappeared. "No."

"Pardon?"

"No, I'm not kind. I'm terrible."

"Oh. I'm sure you're not, but it's not really my place to correct you, is it? So I'm going to go, because, you see—"

The duke broke into her babble. "May I make a suggestion?"

That you kiss me with those dangerous lips? That you put your arms around me? That we both undress, Your Grace, and get back into the bed and you let me get a feel of whatever was prodding my backside for the last ten minutes? That you remind me how wondrous the human body is? And that I'm alive and not just going through the motions in the hopes that everything will work out happily in the end?

The duke blinked several times as if he could read her thoughts.

He cleared his throat. "May I suggest coffee before anything else?"

Six

She was a strange one. Of course, not as strange as he was since no one was as strange as he was, according to his mother and Dagenham, the two people who knew him best. But Franny didn't know anything about a kitchen. Kittredge had to stoke the stove and heat the water and grind the coffee himself.

She stared at him, agog. "A duke knows how to make coffee?"

He shrugged. "I make a point of spending six weeks a year in a hunting box with no servants."

His eye was caught by a pile of his books by the hearth. Curiously, it stirred not a whit of anger in him. *She* was welcome to read his books. Welcome to anything she wanted, really. But how could he convince her to want *him*?

"The first year Dagenham and I nearly starved to death. And we were right ogres to each other with no coffee. The next year I spent two months in this kitchen before we left, learning how to make coffee and eggs and roast a haunch of venison."

"And make toast?"

"There's no such thing as making toast."

"There isn't?"

"No. One buys bread and slices it and then one attempts not to burn the slices of bread. So you see, nothing is made."

"There's bread in the larder. Will you not burn some toast for me, Your Grace?"

He'd do anything she asked of him. He found the loaf and a knife and started sawing off some slices. "What's the rest of your name?"

"Cranwell."

"Miss Franny Cranwell."

"Yes?"

"You don't sound sure."

"No, that's my name, all right."

A horror struck him and turned his knees to jelly. "And it's Miss Cranwell? Not Mrs. Cranwell?"

She ducked her head. Was she smiling? "Miss."

"Miss Frances Cranwell."

"Francesca."

Of course. Of course, she was a Francesca and not a Frances.

He looked around and spied a pot of jam but had no idea where a toasting fork might be. He put a kitchen cloth over his arm and brought over the board with the bread on it and the pot of jam.

"I call this raw toast. It's a special dish I invented just for you."

Her gap-toothed grin and the remarkable laugh. "Yes. Very special."

He poured them both coffee and sat across from her, just as he had on the stage coach.

In between bites of bread and jam, she asked, "Why are you here?"

"It's my house."

She giggled, spraying crumbs. "I'm asking how you came to be in London. You're meant to be at a house party."

"I ran away."

"Why?"

"Young ladies of the *ton* hate me."

"That's the most ridiculous thing I've ever heard."

He nodded. "And yet it's true."

"I don't hate you."

"You're not one of them."

"But they're just like me, aren't they? Just several years younger."

"Not at all like you."

"Untrue!"

"What do you know about daughters of dukes and marquesses?"

She straightened up. "I know they're perfectly nice girls, that's all. And they don't go around hating people."

"What are you?"

"Pardon?"

"We agree you're not a young lady. So what are you? And who is Mrs. Tumney and how are you related to her?"

Her jaw dropped. "You don't know who Mrs. Tumney is?"

"No."

"She's your cook. She's been your cook for months."

"Oh."

She whispered, "You really *are* terrible."

He had unwittingly crawled into bed with her and held her tightly and rubbed his cockstand against her perfect arse— basically, he had mauled her while he was asleep—and it took not knowing his cook's name for her to believe he was terrible?

"I warned you."

"Y-yes," she faltered. "But I thought it was polite hyperbole."

"I'm not polite. And hyperbole? It's the equivalent of a Christmas house party. I detest both and partake in neither. How do you know my cook?"

"She used to be the cook…I mean…I was…I'm a companion."

She had just skirted telling him something. But he'd worm it out of her eventually. He could be a ruthless wormer. "A companion to whom?"

"Lady LeClere."

"Poor you."

"Stop! She's very nice."

Franny had crumbs resting on the shelf her pretty breasts made. Could he reach out and brush off the crumbs and get close to those irresistible soft scoops of flesh?

No. Keep your hands to yourself. And say something. It's your turn.

"Nice? Just like the young ladies?"

"Yes! She's very sweet. Look how she let me come away for Christmas to see Mrs. Tumney and my brother."

"She let you come alone on a stage coach."

Franny laughed and tossed her head. "What's wrong with a stage coach? I hear even dukes are taking them nowadays."

"Lady LeClere or your brother should have arranged a private post-chaise for you. Or your brother should have come to fetch you himself. And Lady LeClere keeps you in old boots."

She looked down at her feet. Her face went red. Wait. Had he shamed her?

Damn.

She bit her lower lip. "My brother is in school. He's only thirteen. And my boots are my fault. I use my money for other things."

"Like pies for people you don't know?"

Her chagrin fled, and she looked at him, eyes flashing, fierce and bold. "Yes. It's my money."

He blew on his coffee. "I'm very careful with my money. If you like, I could show you the way I keep track of my expenditures. Give you some advice on sound investments."

She said nothing at first. Then she laughed. "Men always want to fix things. Especially me."

He felt unaccountably angry. "For good or ill, you'll find quickly I am not *men*, Miss Cranwell. And I have no desire to fix you. I just want you to be properly shod." He was practically shouting. He forced himself to take a swallow of his coffee.

She tilted her head to the side, not daunted in the least. "You really don't want to fix me? You really don't want to tell me I'm terribly impractical and I laugh too much and eat too much jam?"

"No."

"That's astonishingly lovely. You're astonishingly lovely."

His face felt hot. He was not *lovely*. Whatever he was, it was not *lovely*. But…how lovely that she thought he was.

He blustered to cover the borehole she had driven straight into his chest. "And if you were my companion, I'd buy you new boots."

She smirked. "Dukes don't have companions."

"No. They have mistresses."

He studied her reaction to what he had just said. She narrowed her eyes and studied him back.

Then she shook her head *no*. Just an inch back and forth. Ah, well. There went that possibility. He shouldn't have held any hope. A woman who used her money for pies for strangers instead of new boots would not be interested in his gifts of jewelry in exchange for putting up with him.

She brushed the breadcrumbs off her bosom herself and licked a bit of jam from the corner of her mouth. "Dukes shouldn't have mistresses. They should have wives. A wife. A duchess."

He buried his face in his hands and groaned. "You sound like my mother."

"She must be a brilliant woman."

"She is."

"Then why are you such a—"

He lifted his head, held his breath, waiting for the *arsehole*. It didn't come.

"—silly thing? I'm sure all those poor women at the house party are devastated you aren't attending."

"I told you. As soon as they met me, they would hate me."

"Oh. You were being serious. I thought you were trying to be funny."

"I don't do that."

"What?"

"Try to be funny."

"Are you averse to trying or to being funny?"

"I have no sense of humor."

"Bosh. Everybody has a sense of humor."

He shrugged and took a sip of coffee.

"Raw toast. That's a sense of humor, Kit."

"It is?"

THE POOR MAN. Thinking he had no sense of humor. Thinking people hated him. And he was so sweet. Making her coffee and raw toast. A duke, making her coffee!

And he wasn't charming. Not a bit. And that was intensely charming to Franny who was done with the other kind of charming for the rest of her life. And he had those hungry storm-tossed ocean-blue eyes and he was so handsome whether he was smiling or scowling or stoic. Even in a shabby tweed coat covered in dog hair.

Without thinking, she reached out and pulled a hank of brown fur off the lapel of his coat.

Oh, no. She stood, bumping the table, spilling her coffee into the saucer.

"The dog!"

"What about him?"

"He hasn't been out since last night."

He shrugged. "If Bevel needed to go out, he'd be down here, barking."

How could he be so calm? "Well, where is he?"

"Would you feel better if we found him?"

"Yes." She started towards the stairs.

"Stay."

A harsh command issued by a man who expected obedience. What the Helen-of-Troy? She whirled around. She had an inkling of an idea now about the *young-ladies-hate-me* thing.

He scowled. "What's wrong, Miss Cranwell?"

She folded her arms. "Never talk to me like that again."

"Like what?"

"Like I'm the dog."

"I didn't." He put two fingers in his mouth and emitted a piercing whistle. "*That's* how I talk to Bevel."

Sure enough, within a few seconds, she could hear Bevel coming down the stairs. No further apology was forthcoming from the duke. The man must think none was needed.

But she had a question she hadn't asked before and now she was dying to know the answer. "Why's his name Bevel?"

He shook his head.

"No, tell me, please."

"He takes the sharp edges off, smooths me down," he muttered.

"Maybe you should take him to meet the young ladies with you."

"Women don't like big dogs."

"Bosh and bollocks."

"Refined and proper women don't like big dogs." He looked at her. "What are you shaking your head about?"

The silly man was not even aware he had just insulted her. Yet another part of the problem slotted into place.

The dog trotted into the kitchen and the duke opened the door to the mews. Bevel sat and looked at him until he closed the door.

"I told you he didn't need to go out."

"Yes, you were right."

Her admission made his lips curve upwards again as he closed the door. There, the dimples.

"You have dimples."

"Yes."

"They're quite becoming. Have you ever shown your dimples to a possible future duchess?"

"No."

"Oh-ho. I see. You're a serious, brooding rake, not a joking, roguish one."

He folded his arms in front of his chest. "What do you know about rakes?"

She waved her hand airily. "I've met my share."

Was that a snarl coming from him? "I'm not a rake. I'm whatever the opposite is."

"I thought all dukes were rakes."

"I'm not like other dukes."

"No. You're very special and very lovely."

"Stop saying that." His face was red.

"What?" She knew, but he was such fun to tease.

"*Lovely*. You make me feel like a fraud. I'm not lovely."

"You're so wrong. You couldn't be more wrong." She made a decision. She slapped her hand down on the table. "I have a proposition for you, Your Grace. What do you say to letting me stay here in your house for a bit?"

Far too quickly, almost as he had given it previous thought, he said, "I say yes."

"I'm not finished. And in exchange for letting me *and* my brother stay here for a jolly Christmas in London, I'll help you with your problem."

"My problem?"

"Your young lady problem."

SEVEN

He desperately needed time alone. For relief and to shore up his ongoing success at not acting like a slavering brute. He couldn't believe how well he was doing so far, and he didn't want to press his luck.

"I'm going upstairs, Miss Cranwell. For clean clothes."

She chewed on her bottom lip, and her brows came together.

"What's wrong?" Good God, he'd never asked that question of a woman before, and now he'd asked it twice in one morning.

"I've been in my stays for over a day. Fell asleep without taking them off. Would you mind… that is, would it bother you if I removed them?"

Every bit of blood in his head rushed to his cock, and all he saw was red. Red nipples. His mouth went dry, and his lips stuck to his teeth. Air could not enter his lungs.

But still, he tried to sound as if he discussed women's undergarments, or the lack of them, all the time. "No. It wouldn't bother. Me."

It came out as a growl. But better that than a whimper.

She smiled and nodded her head as if he had agreed to take tea with her next week. "Lovely."

As he attended to himself in his dressing room, his mind was full of Franny two staircases below him. In her stays and a chemise. He saw Franny reaching behind to untie the knot of the lace of her stays.

No. Instead, it was him untying and looking down over her shoulder at the tops of her breasts. She let out a moan of pleasure once the lace was loosened and he had drawn the stays off and over her head.

She arched her spine as she leaned back against him, her head resting on his chest, her arms going up and coming around the back of his neck, giving him the access he wanted. He wrapped his arms around her to cup her breasts, to lift and knead, his thumbs running over her hardening nipples under her chemise.

As his hand moved more quickly over his cock, his fantasy accelerated in the nonsensical way his fantasies always did. She was naked. Both of them were naked. Her nipples *were* red. Saucy little things poking out, impudently erect. His waist was girdled by her legs, his hands gripped her heavenly bottom, his cock was deep in her hot, wet cunt. He plopped her on top of the bread crumbs on the kitchen table. He took her with hard thrusts, and she screamed, "Kit, Kit, Kit, Kit—"

Finished. He panted. He'd made a mess like a boy. But he'd clean up and get dressed now. He had a chance of behaving well for a few hours longer. Or what passed as behaving well for him.

In the library, he opened the drapes and built a fire to warm the room. She joined him and began pacing up and down in front of the windows.

Stayless.

My God, he couldn't take his eyes off her. He was spellbound by the jouncing oscillation of her breasts. Again, his mind went to her nipples and…damn. His cock was acting as if he hadn't just stroked himself to completion ten minutes ago.

"How old are you?" he asked to keep himself from asking about the color of her nipples.

"Oh, goodly gosling. You interrupted my train of thought."

"I did?" People did that to him all the time. He hadn't realized he could do it to other people. Dagenham and Bevel had no trains of thought as far as he could tell.

"Yes, you did. I was trying to decide where to start your schooling. You implied your mother wants you to be married. Is that true?"

"Don't you know it's the wish of all mothers? You must not have one yourself."

The look on her face. He had said something wrong.

"I don't," she said and turned away.

"Of course you have a mother. It's a necessity."

"Yes, but she died."

"I see."

A long silence hung between them. But it wasn't his turn.

She turned and shook a finger at him. "What should you say next?"

What was the woman on about?

She folded her arms. "If I were a young lady and you had just discovered my mother was dead, what would you say next to me?"

"I said *I see*. That's a safe thing to say. Now it's your turn."

"It's not safe. It's unfeeling. You should say *I have the deepest sympathy for your loss*."

He made a choking sound. "Really?"

"Yes. Or, if I were a young lady to whom you wanted to propose marriage, you could say something more intimate. You might say *perhaps you'll have a larger family soon*. No, no, you would say *I have no doubt you yourself will be a wonderful mother*. Don't make that face!"

He had no idea he was making a face. "What face?"

"That sour face."

"That's my regular face."

"No, it isn't. It's the first time I've seen it. Even when you were angry yesterday when that other man sat next to me, you didn't look sour. Just rageful. Let me ask you this—do *you* want to get married?"

"Yes."

"But you think women hate you."

"I'm an arsehole. Everyone knows it."

"I don't know it." She came closer and peered at him. "I think you're scrumptious."

Scrumptious? She said it like it was a compliment. "I think you need spectacles."

She backed away. "You shouldn't be so critical of yourself."

"I'm not. I said that because of how close you hold a book to your face."

"Oh."

"Believe me, I know my looks are not my problem."

She laughed her remarkable laugh. "Oh, you do, do you?"

"Women often say I'm handsome before they get to know me," he said stiffly. "Do you think so?"

"I think you're kind. Protective. Helpful. Look how you saved me in the stage coach from that appalling man. How you made me breakfast."

"But do you think I'm handsome?" he persisted.

She put her fists on her waist, arms akimbo, giving him his best view yet of her stayless breasts. "I think even plain men can get wives. Plain, portly, bald men who are not dukes. Being handsome is not important."

Frustrated, he threw himself into a wing chair.

"You're a case in point, Kit."

Aha! He sprang up. "So you do think I'm handsome."

"I didn't say that."

"You implied it when you said I was a case in point. Meaning I was the case where being handsome was not of importance in getting married because I'm handsome and not married."

She tilted her head and scrutinized him. "Do you like winning arguments?"

"Of course."

"Do you ever let anyone else win?"

"No."

"Which would you prefer—to win every argument or to be married?"

"I can't have both?"

The remarkable laugh filled the room.

THIS MAN. Oh, this darling, absolute love of a man. So funny, so dear, so sweet, and he had no idea whatsoever.

Finally, she got her laughter under control.

"All right, Your Grace. Let's say you can't have both."

"I don't mind losing an argument if I'm wrong."

"And are you always right?"

"Very close to always."

She had to laugh again.

He scowled at her. "What are you laughing at?"

"You're…you're…" She couldn't get the breath to finish her sentence.

"Such an arsehole?"

"No. You're so certain. And I'm not. A will-of-the-wisp, my brother says."

"When is your brother coming?"

"On Christmas Eve. We don't have much time for your lessons, you see, so what will it be? Marriage or win?"

"All right." He sighed. "I'd rather be married than win every argument."

"Good."

He held up a finger. "Because winning all your battles is not the greatest good. The greatest good comes from breaking your enemy's resistance with no battle. Master Sun, *The Art of War.*"

She'd never heard of Mr. Masterson or *The Art of War.* "In your view, young women are the enemy?"

"Yes."

"And lovemaking is war?"

He gulped. "We're not talking about you giving me lessons in lovemaking, are we?"

"Yes."

Suddenly, the feral look from the stage coach was back. "I don't need lessons in that. I'll have you know I'm not a virgin."

Oh, that's why he gulped. Such a delicious, darling dunderhead.

"I didn't think otherwise," she assured him. "Of course, you're not. I'm not, either. And I didn't mean—"

"You're not?"

"No, I'm not. You see, I meant—"

"You're fallen?"

This would not stand. No matter how much she had thought him a darling moments ago. Absolutely not.

"I have a body. Which has desires just like yours. I will never marry, so if I wanted to know the pleasure of sharing a bed, it had to be outside of marriage. I will not be called fallen or ruined or spoiled. I have betrayed no one. Not even God."

He stared at her.

"I'm just like you, Kit. But with breasts. As you've noticed."

He looked away from her.

"And if you want me to stay here, you'll need to apologize to me, Your Grace."

"Yes."

"Now," she snapped.

"I apologize, Franny," he said quickly.

She took a deep breath and tried to get rid of her anger. Unfortunately, the dim duke did not know when to leave off.

"But if you're not an innocent and you won't be getting married, why won't you be my mistress?"

She closed her eyes and held up her hand. *Breathe, sweet girl. He doesn't know what he's saying. Breathe and explain it to him. Find out if he's teachable. And if he's not, run as fast as you can.*

She opened her eyes. "I would never trade affection for money or security. And if you believe that's what a wife does, you're wrong and have no idea what marriage is, and I will not assist you any further in finding a wife."

He looked away and then back at her. There were all kinds of mysterious things going on behind his eyes.

"All right," he said finally.

"And when I said lovemaking, I wasn't speaking about coupling. I meant falling in love."

Now the poor man looked even more uncomfortable than he had when he had thought she was talking about rutting.

"I don't need, I mean," he faltered. "That's not necessary, either. I don't need lessons in that."

"You've been in love before?"

"No."

"Surely, you don't think I would encourage you to marry someone you didn't love? It would be a dreadful mistake."

She knew how dreadful. Such a narrow escape she had had.

"That's what's usually done."

"Nonsense. There are plenty of love matches. In fact, my parents were madly in love—"

"Yes, *your* parents. Not peers."

She sat down heavily. It was her own fault. She'd brought it up. Now she'd have to tell him.

"My father *was* a peer."

Eight

There was loud pounding coming from somewhere.

Franny's father was a peer?

Bevel was barking and a voice was shouting, "Kittredge? Are you in there?"

"Someone's at your door, Your Grace."

Franny was a peer's daughter.

"You need to answer it."

Oh, yes. There was no butler. But a peer's daughter? Well…then…he could marry *her*, couldn't he?

He sensed he had been very close to being called an arsehole, but she hadn't said that yet, so there was still hope, wasn't there? He should ask her right now before he said something unforgivable.

"Franny, will you ma—"

The pounding suddenly became ten times louder, and Bevel's bark in the front hall was ear-splitting.

Franny got up from her chair and went out into the hall, and Kittredge came behind her quickly as she opened the door. He must get his question out.

"Whoa, boy! Enough!" It was Dagenham's voice. Bevel went quiet, and Franny stepped back.

"Kittredge!" Dagenham came in and fondled Bevel's ears. "You found him. You could have sent me word. I've been worried."

"You have?"

"Well, I was about to get worried." Dagenham's eyes slid over to Franny as she closed the door, and he swept off his hat. "Good day."

Dagenham had said women often liked him. He knew how to flatter and flirt. He had a sly intelligence despite his stupid gambling habit. If Dagenham weren't so atrociously poor, he'd be one of the most sought-after bachelors in the *ton*.

Dagenham bowed. "I won't wait forever for Kittredge to remember his manners and introduce us. It's been many years, uh, Miss Cranwell."

Franny curtsied. "Lord Dagenham."

Kittredge didn't like this. "You two know each other?"

Franny looked from Kittredge to Dagenham and back again. She raised her chin defiantly.

"Yes, we met during my Season. When I was still Lady Francesca Cranwell. "

She walked away, towards the back of the house, Bevel trotting along beside her.

"Have anything to warm up a fellow?" Dagenham rubbed his hands together and strode into the library.

Mutely, Kittredge followed. Dagenham went over to a decanter on top of a pile of books.

"I don't understand," Kittredge finally got out.

"That must be very discomfiting for you. I don't understand what she's doing in your house, so we both don't understand something."

"Why was she Lady Francesca before and now she's not?"

Dagenham chuckled and sat in front of the fire with his glass. "You don't remember the scandal when the Marquess of Merrifield died last year?"

Kittredge had no interest in *ton* scandals. And he couldn't remember what he had never known.

Dagenham crossed his legs and balanced his hat on one knee. "The marquess was her father. His marchioness was the daughter of some Italian count. She died giving birth to the son, I think. Then, after the marquess died, it came out they had never been married by a Church of England clergyman. Only by a Catholic priest in Italy. Lady Francesca and her brother were declared illegitimate. The brother was stripped of the title and since everything was entailed, they haven't a sixpence to rub together. They lost it all."

Kittredge was overwhelmed by his own profound loss.

His grief.

For a few seconds, he'd had a possible wife within his grasp. A daughter of even the lowliest baron could be potentially polished up into a duchess. And Franny was a woman who tolerated him. A woman whom he wanted to touch and to bed and to…oh, all kinds of things that didn't even have to do with a bed. He wanted to make her laugh. Make her raw toast. Tickle her. Absurd.

And now his wife was gone.

Franny was a by-blow, and he could never marry her. Dukes didn't marry bastards. Nobody with a title did. No wonder Franny said she'd never marry.

Dagenham shot Kittredge a quizzical look. "And you were going to the Christmas rout of the current Marquess of Merrifield?"

Kittredge grunted.

Dagenham grimaced. "What hideous irony. The marquess is Lady Francesca's former betrothed. Used to be a baronet. Sir Michael Sempleton."

"Really?"

"Yes. His estate adjoined the Merrifield march. And he was engaged to Lady Francesca for years and years. Broke it off when her father died and then went and petitioned his pal Prinny to have the title transferred to him since otherwise it would go extinct."

"What?"

"Yes. Rumor has it he somehow knew the children weren't legitimate and he got engaged to Lady Francesca just to get close to the family and make sure the father didn't remarry and produce a legitimate heir. The Semp never intended to marry her, at all. He was just waiting for the father to die so he could grab the title. And he spread it all around she'd granted him unmentionable liberties. Now. You do some explaining. Why's she here?"

"She's friends with my cook," Kittredge mumbled and went over to the decanter. He needed whisky. A large amount. He poured himself a tumbler full and drank half of it in one enormous gulp. Then he was coughing and Dagenham was at his side, thumping him on his back.

"Easy there. Looks like she's friends with Bevel, too."

Kittredge finally recovered himself. "Stop hitting me. Yes. He likes her."

"And you?" Dagenham grinned. "She's very pretty, Kittredge. A lively little chit. I always thought she was far too good for the Semp. She might be—"

"What? What might she be?"

"She might be a nice woman for you to get to know."

Kittredge took a threatening step towards Dagenham. "What do you mean by that?"

"Easy, easy, easy. I don't mean anything. I just…it's nice she's in your house, that's all. It's nice for you to have the chance to converse with a woman."

"I've conversed with plenty of women."

Dagenham raised his brows.

"All right," Kittredge said. "I haven't. And you're right. It is nice to have her in the house."

Dagenham staggered back in mock-horror. "Kittredge concedes a point!"

"I'm learning to. From Miss Cranwell."

Dagenham's tone was one of disbelief. "You're learning something. From Miss Cranwell."

"Yes. It's a barter. She gets to stay here while she's in London. And in return, she's going to help me woo a wife. Apparently, I'm not meant to win every argument."

Dagenham groaned. "Something I've told you a million times before, you daft clunch."

Kittredge waved his hand in dismissal. Of course, Dagenham had said that before, but that was because Dagenham was tired of always losing. Cards. Dice. Arguments with Kittredge.

Dagenham drained his glass. "Well, good luck with your tempting armful of a teacher. I hope you can keep your attention where it should be. Will you call Bevel for me or should I go get him?"

"Bevel's staying here. With me. Your duty is done."

Dagenham smirked. "You're going to stay here. With Bevel. And Miss Cranwell. I see."

"You see what?"

"Nothing. I'm sure Bevel is an ideal chaperone." Dagenham headed towards the front hall. "Happy Christmas, Kittredge. I hope you get everything you want."

Kittredge would never get everything he wanted.

He wanted Franny.

And he could never have her.

NINE

One more large whisky gave Kittredge some solace before he went and found Franny in the kitchen with her coat on, wrapping her muffler around her neck. Bevel was whining.

"Here. Where are you going?"

Franny looked down as she put on her gloves. "I don't know yet."

He saw her reticule and satchel on the table. She was leaving.

"I'm sure you learned my history from Lord Dagenham. I was about to tell you. I'm sorry."

He hiccoughed. "Don't be sorry. You didn't have anything to do with your parents not getting married properly."

Franny sighed and looked up at him. Her eyes were beautiful. Deep and soulful. The warmest brown imaginable. A very dark amber. A midnight honey. The color of a priceless aged whisky.

He staggered. He was half-sprung.

"I didn't set out to deceive you. I just…" She shrugged. "I was tired of people whispering behind my back and speaking to me with condescending pity. I just adored being with you and how you treated me like I was a person."

You are a person, he tried to say. But *I adored being with you* reverberated like an enormous bell in his head. Instead what came out was, "You must hate your father for not making sure of everything for you and your brother."

Because *he* hated her father, a man he had never met. For ruining his, Kittredge's, future marriage to this woman he craved with every bit of his being.

Her face went red. "Never. I could never hate him. Yes, *Papà* was rather careless with everything. But not his love. He was a fourth son and resented his title when all he ever wanted to do was paint."

"Well, I don't want you to leave because you're a bastard. I want you to stay. I want you to have your Christmas. I want my schooling. How to lose an argument. All that."

She shook her head and picked up the satchel and reticule and walked to the door.

"Please, Franny." He was so dizzy. He collapsed into a chair. "I need you."

The kitchen was very quiet except for the sound of Bevel slobbering. Franny paused with her hand on the latch.

"You need me?" Her voice was strained.

Had he unwittingly stumbled on the right thing to say? "Yes. Yes. I need you. And not just to show me how to court a young lady, but also…but also…"

What would make her stay? *Think, you tipsy idiot.* Oh. Yes. Franny loved Christmas. She had said so in the stage coach.

"Because, otherwise, I'll be all alone for Christmas. Just me and Bevel. I'd rather have Christmas with you. And your brother. A proper Christmas."

She turned around, and he tried his best to assume a pathetic expression. He certainly *felt* pathetic.

"You hate Christmas," she said.

"No. I hate Christmas house parties."

"Well, it will be Christmas. And this is a house. And—"

"Yes. But three—well, Bevel makes four—that's not a real party, is it? More of a small gathering."

Her lips pouted. Oooh. He hadn't seen a pout on her. Those *lips*.

She spoke through her pout. "And you have no objections to Christmas house small gatherings?"

"None. None whatsoever."

She stepped away from the door and unwrapped her muffler. "I'll stay for Christmas."

Thank God. But he'd better warn her of his ignorance. "Of course, I don't know how to do it."

"You don't know how to do Christmas?"

"No."

She clucked her tongue and unbuttoned her coat, laughing. "Poor Kit. The little lost duke."

She had seen through his pathetic act. But she was still staying. And wasn't that even better? She was staying because she wanted to and not because she felt sorry for him.

He smiled at her. Broadly.

In fact, the Duke of Kittredge grinned like a besotted fool. Because he was one.

"Obviously, Your Grace got a bit bosky in the time it took me to get my stays laced up again—"

His eyes dropped to her breasts, and he cursed under his breath. The stays were back on.

"—so I think we should have something to eat besides raw toast. You have to be steady on your feet for your next lesson." Her face lit up. "I saw something scrumptious in the larder."

She disappeared into the larder. So *scrumptious* wasn't his word. It didn't belong to him, just like *lovely* didn't. But that faded into a minor grievance when a beaming Franny came back into the kitchen with a crock of iced biscuits.

Ten

She had been waltzing with him for the last hour in the music room, training Kit to say the polite nothings his future dance partners would expect.

He kept impeccable time. He was surprisingly graceful. Those commanding fingers she had first encountered in the stage coach curled around her waist and clasped her hand as he moved her around the room with flawless control.

He was definitely the best waltzer Franny had ever partnered. She felt like a piece of floating gossamer when she'd always been a dancer possessed of more enthusiasm than skill.

A socially awkward man with no physical awkwardness. He was probably an excellent lover.

She giggled just as he complimented her dress.

"What's wrong with what I said?" He frowned and guided her away from certain collision with the pianoforte while continuing his perfect *one-two-three*. "I repeated exactly what you told me to say."

"Yes, you did. And you looked right into my eyes and seemed quite sincere. First-rate."

"So why did you laugh?"

"You're a very good dancer. Why is that?"

"I had lessons. I'm a good pupil, and the better I did, the sooner the lessons were over, and I could do something I liked."

"You're a marvel. Most people can't be good at something they don't like."

He brought her to a stop slowly but didn't release her. "So I dance well?"

"Very well."

"How was my conversation?"

"Passable."

"What's next?"

"Kissing."

Suddenly her back was against the music room's priceless mural. Kit crowded her with his body, each of his enormous hands flat on the painted wall on both sides of her head, his arms caging her in. His breath, sweet with whisky and ginger biscuits, warmed her face. She tipped her chin up and forced herself to meet his eyes. Those wild, hungry eyes.

"Franny." His voice was deep and rough. "I want to kiss you. Let me kiss you now."

A beast out of nowhere. Like in the coach with that dreadful man. Like when I said I wanted to take off my stays. Like when he thought I was talking about rutting.

She kept her voice light. "That's only natural. When was the last time you kissed anyone?"

"I haven't been with a woman in two years and ten months."

"So, no wonder. We're in close proximity. Alone in the house. And we've been practicing courtship. But I really think you shouldn't have your arms like that."

He turned his head, looking at each of his arms as if they weren't part of him before returning his gaze to her face.

She must explain. "You might scare the poor girl, Your

Grace. You must give her every opportunity to get away from you if she wants to."

"You're not scared."

"No."

"And you won't run away?"

"I won't."

He slowly lowered his arms to his sides.

"But I think telling her you want to kiss her is a very good start."

He said nothing but continued to stare at her like she was a lamb and he was a starving wolf.

"But what you're saying and how you behave have to match."

He shook his head, telling her he didn't understand.

"You say you want to kiss me, but you're acting like you want to tup me."

"I do want to tup you."

Her breath caught. A throb started up between her legs. *Say something. Anything besides I want to tup you, too.*

She coughed into her fist. "Of course, you do. You're a man in your prime, and you haven't had coitus in years. You'd want to tup anyone with breasts, I warrant." He tried to break in here, but she wouldn't let him. "However, a young lady doesn't know about tupping, Kit."

"You do."

"I'm beside the point. When you kiss a young lady, you must be concentrating on the kiss. Only the kiss. Nothing more advanced. At least for the first kiss. You must make the first kiss just a kiss. And wonderful."

His feral look faded away, and a haze came over him. She was losing him to that mysterious place he went sometimes.

"Kit!"

He blinked.

"Kit, do you like kissing?"

His spine went rigid. "I've never thought about it."

"You like what the kissing leads to?" And even though she knew it was dangerous, she winked at him.

Franny, you are so naughty. Stop flirting. Right now.

He answered her question quickly. Seriously. "Yes."

"You know the answer to that question right away. Which means you're comparatively indifferent to kissing."

Suddenly, his hands were on her waist, and he was pulling her into him. "I wouldn't be indifferent to kissing you."

Oh, mirthiful elevens. The ridge of his hardness was against her belly. She felt her own wildness rising to the surface, bubbling, boiling, the desire, the want, the raw need. What would it be like to have this gorgeous, ravenous madman bed her? Gadzooks.

She steeled herself. "Let go."

He did immediately, and she almost whimpered, almost threw herself back up against him. But instead she stepped away and put her hands behind her to keep herself from touching his hair, his jaw, his shoulders, the beautiful bulge in his breeches.

"I'm going to teach you how to kiss an innocent young lady, Kit. Not me. Is that clear?"

A wily look. "But it's you I'll be kissing, correct?"

"Yes."

"So…" He moved several inches closer to her.

She took another step away. "So. A kiss speaks without words. What do you think a first kiss should say?"

He rolled his eyes.

"Guess, Kit."

"Well, now I know it shouldn't say I want to fu— I mean, tup you."

"Good, yes. But what *should* it say?"

. . .

HE HAD no idea what a kiss should say. He very much needed to adjust himself inside his breeches, but he couldn't in front of Franny. "You tell me."

A small smile came to those lips he was dying to ravish. She was thinking about past kisses, damn it.

"A first kiss should say *you're beautiful*."

"You *are* beautiful."

"Hush." But her face was a little rosier than it had been before. "A first kiss should say *I cherish you*. It should say *I adore you* and *you're the only woman for me*."

All that? A large bundle of things for a simple pressing together of two mouths. No kiss could bear that burden.

But there was even more, apparently.

"It should promise you'll be careful with her. Her heart. Her spirit. Her body."

He couldn't stop himself from asking. "Was your first kiss like that? With the Semp?"

She was startled. "With whom?"

"Sir Michael Sempleton. Or, should I say, Lord Merrifield?"

She sucked her lower lip into her mouth. Damn, damn, damn. Why had he mentioned the man who had jilted her and now held what should have been her brother's title?

She surprised him by laughing.

"Oh, no. He wasn't my first kiss. I was a horrible flirtabout. Had kissed dozens of boys before him."

He exhaled. Surely, the Duke of Kittredge could compete with boys.

"But, no, my first kiss ever wasn't like that. But my sixth kiss was."

"With whom?"

"Someone who was far too old for me and should have known better. Especially since he was already married."

He felt fury at the greedy sack-of-shit who had kissed Franny when he already had a wife. "So you want to teach me to kiss like some faithless scoundrel?"

She stepped forward and took both his hands, forcing his fists to relax as her fingers wove into his.

"Kit, if that man had asked me to run away with him right after his kiss, I would have. If a sincere bachelor with good intentions could kiss like that, he could have any girl he wanted."

Her hands calmed him. And her words. Sincere. Good intentions. That's what she thought of him. How little she knew. He took a deep breath. "I'm ready."

She shook her head. "No. We have to go out first. We need to go shopping."

"For what?"

"Mistletoe."

Eleven

As they walked, she explained she had decided she should no longer dally. "No more kissing, flirting, getting entangled. I have to be responsible for my brother's sake. I must keep my position."

I'd like to keep you in all kinds of positions, Franny. He stuffed his thumbs into his fists and cracked his knuckles, willing his besmirched mind to behave.

"You said I was going to kiss you."

"Yes. Under mistletoe. Then it's all right. Just part of Christmas. Harmless."

"So," he said slowly, to make sure he understood. "Kissing under mistletoe is harmless."

"Yes."

Kittredge would have snorted in derision if anyone else had asserted this, but he was happy Franny suffered this delusion.

She patted his arm. "That's why everyone does it."

"I don't do it."

"If you want a kissing lesson, you will." She gave him a wink, along with a pout.

Minx.

Franny led him east and a little south. He rarely walked in the city. Walking was for the country. But the air seemed fresh today for London. Lots of people bustled down the streets, carrying parcels of various kinds. And he liked having Franny on his arm and listening to her talk about her brother and her plans for Christmas.

"—sad, thinking he needs to be taking care of me when he's only a boy. And he works so hard at school, always studying. He needs to have fun this Christmas. We'll have to play games—"

Kittredge was *not* playing games.

"—and decorate and music, too. Oh, I wish I played the pianoforte!"

"I play."

"You do? Wonderful! How clever you are, Kit. That'll be lovely. Ren and I can dance, and we'll all sing carols. But I know he'll be disappointed not to see Mrs. Tumney. Oh, no."

She stopped dead in the middle of the crowded pavement, so he had to stop, too.

"Food! Pudding and cakes and trifle and, oh, ever so much more! Ren is a growing boy, and he needs a lot to eat, I should think." She put a gloved finger up to her mouth. "And it must be Christmas food."

A fellow knocked into Franny, pushing her against Kittredge's chest, and his arms came up instinctively and held her close.

"Here, now!" Kittredge shouted, but the lout was long gone, disappearing into the crowd of shoppers, and he would rather concentrate on the delight of having Franny pressed against him.

"Well," she said, pushing away, ending the embrace much too soon. She took his arm, and they began walking again.

"Mrs. Tumney left all kinds of things in the larder, but I would, I mean, I have no idea how to cook."

He grunted. "I cook."

"Yes, I know you do, but this is Christmas dinner. It has to be truly special. Not eggs—and what was it? A haunch of venison? With raw toast for pudding?" She giggled.

How hard could it be? "I can cook a Christmas dinner."

"Really?" She gazed up at him, her eyes shining. "Would you really do that for Ren? I mean, I'll eat Christmas dinner, too, of course, but I want it for him."

He'd be doing it for *her*, but she didn't need to know that. "Ren is an odd name."

"It's short for Laurence. Lorenzo."

"Lorenzo, Ren. Francesca, Franny. Too bad my name doesn't shorten well." The boys at his school had called him Rosie even though he should have been Swanford since he was Marquess of Swanford, his courtesy title before his father died.

"Oh, no," she said and almost stopped again, but he tugged her along. "All this time, I've been calling you Kit, thinking your name was Christopher. But you're Kittredge. It's your title. And of course, I should really be calling you Your Grace. Oh, I'm dreadful."

"Dreadful," he agreed.

"You have to tell me your real name."

"Ambrose."

"Ambrose." She said it as if she was savoring the word. "It's a lovely name."

He snorted. Then, "I prefer you call me Kit."

"Why?"

"Makes me feel different."

"Oh, good." She squeezed his arm. "I'll keep calling you Kit if you like it."

He snorted again. He was not about to tell her how much he liked it. How much he liked *her*. Although he had already confessed that this morning, hadn't he? When he had still been half-asleep, his cock half-hard, and her with her hair falling down and a crease in her cheek from the pillow.

At the Covent Garden market, Franny quickly found a stall selling greenery. Kit stood back and watched her talk to the man, asking where he came from, the ages of his children.

His mind wandered to past Christmastides. Out at Harton Grove, the Pembroke family seat. Yes, he supposed they had eaten large meals. And there must have been holly and fir branches about. He remembered some toys he had received as a child. But he couldn't remember any excitement like Franny's. His Christmases had no connection to hers.

"Kit?" She was touching his arm, a sprig of mistletoe in her hand.

"That's all you're buying?"

"You only need a bit for it to count."

"But I thought you would want a lot of branches and such. For decking the halls. I'm paying. Part of our bargain. Part of giving Ren his Christmas."

Giving you *Christmas, Franny.*

"Oh, thank you, that will be so lovely. But I want every-thing to be fresh so it will last until Twelfth Night. And it's bad luck to have greenery in the house before Christmas Eve. You must know that."

He had never held with superstition, but clearly Franny did.

"I made Mr. Enys," she flashed a smile at the stallkeeper, "promise to hold back his best holly for me. Lots of red berries. I love red." She took Kittredge's arm and they started walking back the way they had come.

Despite worry about not getting his kissing lesson, her inconsistency nagged at him. "What about the mistletoe? Won't it be bad luck?"

Franny only laughed.

An hour later, Kittredge was disgruntled to find himself in his cold, empty carriage house. He had imagined a kissing lesson on a sofa. Inside, where it was warm. Where they could shed their coats. Where he might see and touch more of her body. But Franny wouldn't take the mistletoe inside the house proper, so they were in the carriage house.

Shut up. Don't complain. You're going to get to kiss her, you lucky cove.

Franny reached up and stuck the sprig of mistletoe in a crack in one of the upright posts.

She turned to face him, standing directly under the little piece of green. Her breath puffed out of her mouth in a white cloud.

"All right. You remember what I said?"

You're beautiful. I cherish you. I adore you. You're the only woman for me. I'll be careful with you. Your heart, your spirit, your body.

And he meant it.

He stepped closer to her and held her shoulders firmly, but not too firmly.

She tilted her chin up at him, eyes big and sparkling, cheeks pink. Her perfect red cupid's bow. Her succulent lower lip, trembling slightly. God, she was more than beautiful.

He pushed away *arsehole* and *clodpole* and *I want to tup you* and kept her words in his mind: *you're beautiful, I cherish you, I adore you.*

He trembled himself now. He turned his head slightly, bent his neck, and put his lips to hers. *You're beautiful, I cherish you, I adore you.*

Her mouth was warm, soft, yielding. Everything he had thought it would be. But better. Because he had felt her heated breath on his chin, filled his nostrils with the fragrance of her skin, heard her swallow right before he kissed her.

Because it was Franny.

He broke the kiss, let go of her, stepped back. Her eyes were closed.

"How was that?"

SHE OPENED HER EYES.

His own blue-gray eyes smoldered. His forehead furrowed questioningly. Those heavenly sculpted lips that had just caressed her with such care were slightly parted.

She should say something.

And it shouldn't be *I'll run away with you right now. Even if it's just upstairs to your bedchamber or back into a horse's stall. I'm yours.*

Although that's what she wanted to say.

"It was very good," she choked out. She made herself smile. "You're a quick study."

"Something must have been wrong with it."

"No, no. It was perfect."

Devil the man. There went a reason to kiss him more. She'd have him engaged to the prettiest virgin of the *ton* by Twelfth Night at this rate.

He glared. "You're quite sure? I don't need to do it again?"

"N-n-no." Drabbit, she was stammering like a green girl.

He shook his head, furious at something, and turned on his heel to go, but she caught his sleeve.

"Wait. Wait. Maybe…maybe you *should* do it again. Just so I can…make sure."

He stopped and turned back to her, his face expressionless. "All right." He took his gloves off and put them in his pocket.

This time he got closer to her. The fronts of their coats brushed together and she could feel the heat coming off his body. His large hands came up and cradled her face reverently. A thumb brushed her cheek.

"That's an improvement already, isn't it?" he said softly.

"Y-y-yes," she admitted.

His face descended, and if the last kiss had been devastating in its sweet gentleness, this kiss was an all-consuming wave of tenderness. He took her mouth and melted it, consuming her lips, tasting them, exploring them. He moved his head, and from another angle, he leaned into her with slightly more pressure.

Her knees weakened. Embers glowed in her belly. The tips of her breasts ached for touch. And between her legs, a slick throb set up a pulse of longing and yearning.

The kiss went on and on and on and there was no haste, there was no cold, there was no sound except the beating of her heart.

He ended the kiss but did not move away, continuing to clasp her face in his warm hands.

She opened her eyes.

"Was that better?" he asked.

He had dissolved her ability to form thoughts. Words. She swallowed. She licked her lips.

"I didn't think it possible, but it was."

"You're a very good teacher, Franny."

A good teacher? She was seconds away from climbing his body like she was the beast he had shown her earlier.

She took an abrupt step to the side, breaking his hold on her face, getting away from him. There could be no more kissing.

She amended. There could be no more kissing *right now*.

"I'll, er, I'll test you again tomorrow. Make sure you don't regress."

Before she could weaken, she went out of the carriage house, out into the gloaming, leaving him standing next to a post sprouting a single twig of mistletoe.

Twelve

Kittredge cursed himself. Why couldn't he have spared a thought for the future? Foreseen that his early success would be the end of kissing?

He was a fool. He should have bungled that first kiss. And the second. Then Franny would have given him another lesson which would have led to more kissing.

More of her lips, her breath whispering over him, her closeness.

But, no. He had to show off how well he had listened. He had to kiss her expertly the first time out. He was a fucking idiot.

It was just as she had said. *Would you rather win or be married?*

He'd rather never win again and spend the rest of his life studying kissing under Franny. Or on top of her.

However, she had agreed the second kiss was even better. He had shown improvement was possible. He would regress tomorrow, and it would be clear he needed an extended period of practice. Advanced kissing lessons.

He left the carriage house. Despite trying to keep tupping

out of his mind, his cock begged for attention, and once he got inside, he went directly to his bedchamber. He was a boy again, ruled by his phallus.

Afterwards, he managed to walk and feed Bevel, slice some pieces off a massive ham in the larder, make some sandwiches, and get through a picnic sort of dinner with Franny.

She had a sheet of foolscap and a pencil and was writing things down as she ate her sandwich and an apple at the kitchen table.

"What's that?"

She looked up, gorgeous, radiant as if lit from within. Had his kisses done that to her?

No.

"I'm making a list of presents I can afford to buy for my brother. And things I want to do with him in London. And things to eat for Christmas. And games to play. And maybe," her eyes glinted mischievously, "what I ought to get *you* for Christmas."

"Should I go get you more paper?"

He was serious, but she laughed.

"I love when you tease me, Kit. So, what do you want for Christmas? What can I get a duke that he doesn't already have?"

"I don't want anything."

She just bent her head to her list again, chortling.

After the washing-up, during which Franny got more soap and water on the floor than on the dishes, they went to the library.

"You don't have many novels," Franny said, running her fingers over spines on the shelves as he closed drapes, lit lamps, and built up the fire.

"I don't. I prefer books with information."

"Novels have information."

He snorted.

"They do," she insisted. "Information about people. All kinds. And the human heart."

He came over to her and pointed. "There are some novels here."

She squinted at the shelf.

He took his spectacles out of his tailcoat pocket. "These were made for me, so they might not help. But try them."

She put them on, and her eyes widened. She looked back at the shelf. "Oh. Oh, Kit. The letters are so crisp. I can read the spines." She turned to him and threw her arms around his neck and bussed him on the cheek.

He was too slow to turn his head and capture her mouth with his, to get his arms around her. She had already let go and turned back to the books.

"I've heard this is funny." She brought down a fat volume he recognized. *Tristram Shandy*.

"That book is utter nonsense."

"Perfect for me." She hugged it to her chest and took off his spectacles and held them out. "Thank you."

"You keep them." He went in his other pocket. "I have a spare." He showed her his other pair.

She bit her lip and looked down and curtsied. "Thank you, Your Grace."

"None of that, now."

She looked up. Embarrassed? No. Just reluctant to take his spectacles even though he didn't need them.

"Listen to me, Franny. It's an accident of birth, having money. And the money has never made me happy before. So, I know now what I want for Christmas. I want to give you things with no fuss and no protest and no *Your Graces*. I want to buy food for a feast. Buy presents for you to give your brother. Buy enough greenery so the house looks like Sherwood Forest. I want extravagance. I doubt I'll ever be interested in Christmas again, so I might as well make this the biggest, bloody Christmas ever."

"I can't let you do that."

"I let you give me a pie."

She frowned. "Only one, though. I wanted to give you two."

"You like giving things, Franny. So give me Christmas. Give the Duke of Kittredge the chance to give. Don't be selfish and keep all the giving to yourself."

She ducked her head and smiled. "All right."

"But I'll take the spectacles back if you don't thank me properly. As Kit."

She looked up. "Thank you, Kit. You're the most generous man I know."

He had hoped for another kiss, but his stomach flipped just as if she had kissed him.

The most generous man I know was lying hyperbole—no, it came from her own generosity. But he didn't care that it wasn't true. He would clutch at any compliment she gave him.

They settled in front of the fire, Bevel at Franny's feet. But Kittredge could not keep his attention on the page. He kept looking up at Franny. She was enormously fetching wearing the spectacles, the firelight gleaming on the lenses while also flecking her hair with gold. Franny laughed, of course, while reading the book, and Kittredge decided he had better reread the ridiculous thing when she was done. Maybe he had missed the point the first time.

It was a long, lonely night in his very big bed with only Bevel for company.

"How old is your brother again?"

"Thirteen."

He looked around at the brightly-painted things in the toy

shop. "Should we really be buying his Christmas presents here?"

Her face fell. "We didn't celebrate last year because *Papà* died, and I think Ren liked the chess set I gave him the year before."

"But tops? Hobbyhorses? He's too old for all this."

"What did you get for Christmas the year you were thirteen?"

"A horse. A real one."

That gained him a glorious Franny laugh. He held his hand out. "Let me take you where we can get him something he'll want."

She put her hand in his and let him lead her out of the toy shop. He liked that she trusted him. And, yes, they were both gloved—hers knit, his leather, he needed to get her some better gloves along with better boots, was there such a thing as red leather?—but her hand felt so good in his. So right.

Outside in the street, she stopped walking. He turned to look back at her, and her face was pointed at the sky.

"Look, Kit. Snow."

Yes, there were a few flakes falling. He stepped closer and gazed right down at her. A snowflake caught in her eyelash. Another landed on her cheek and melted.

Her eyes shifted to his face. "You're standing awfully near," she whispered.

"Yes."

Suddenly she was fleeing, tugging on his hand, pulling him into an alley as she laughed.

"What are we doing?" he protested.

"You're kissing me in the snow."

"I am?"

"Yes." She went in her pocket of her pelisse and pulled out a small, green leaf. "It fell off the twig yesterday. I came prepared."

He unbuttoned his greatcoat and stepped up to her and wrapped it around her. He felt her arms snake around his middle.

"Don't lose the mistletoe," he said.

"Mmmmm. I won't. I like this already." She smiled, and he saw the gap between her front teeth.

"Shhh," he said.

"Why?"

"Because I'm kissing you."

And despite his vow that he would botch the next kiss, he didn't. He couldn't. He wanted her to enjoy the kiss, to mold herself against him, to kiss him back. And she did.

Just before he ended the kiss, he licked the seam of her lips oh-so-very lightly. And she just slightly parted her lips for him as he did so.

Ah. Good God. She must feel his cockstand pressing against her now.

He put his forehead to hers, not letting go of her. "I'm sorry about…"

She smiled. "Your maypole? I'm not. You flatterer, you."

HE TOOK her to a jeweler's.

She looked at him thoughtfully. "Are you buying a ring here for your future duchess?"

"No. We're buying your brother a watch."

She covered her mouth with her hand. "A watch? Oh, no, I can't afford that."

He raised his brows, reminding her.

She took her hand away. "Oh. Oh, yes. No fuss, no protest. Oh, Kit, he'll love it."

He made her select the watch although she wanted him to choose. First, she was looking at the plain ones, but he insisted she pick up and handle the large, gold ones.

"This one looks just like the one *Papà* had," she said under her breath.

"Then that's the one."

"Thank you, Kit. He's going to adore it."

He leaned on the counter as the man wrapped the watch in velvet so it wouldn't get scratched. "Just don't let him take it apart to see how it works. He'll have a devil of a time getting it back together."

"Take it apart? Oh, you're joking."

"No. I took my first three watches apart. Made a mess of them. And got spanked for it. Of course, I was seven."

She giggled. "So naughty. I wish I had known you when you were a boy."

How wonderful it would have been if he'd had a playmate like Franny to tell him nice things about himself. To wear down his sullen moods with her giggles.

But he *had* had exactly that, hadn't he?

He darted a look at Franny who was chatting now with the man. She looked nothing like his mother. A tall, thin, regal duchess. A daughter of a duke, herself.

But appearances aside, Franny and his mother were very alike. His mother had always seen the best in him, encouraged him, teased him, tried to lighten his gravity with her own joy.

He slapped his hand down on the counter. "I need to buy a Christmas gift for my mother."

"Yes, Your Grace." The man bowed and suddenly trays of necklaces and bracelets and rings and and brooches and tiaras and diamonds, pearls, emeralds, rubies were being laid out.

Franny clapped her hands. "Oh, Kit. What fun! You must pick something extravagantly beautiful for her."

"You choose."

"What have you gotten for her before?"

Nothing. He'd never bought his mother a Christmas present. Good God, he was an arsehole.

He shrugged, but Franny pressed him. What colors did his mother wear, what stones did she like?

The man helping them cleared his throat. "Her Grace honored us two years ago when she asked us to adjust the band on a ruby ring. Her fingers had become narrower, she said, and she was afraid of losing it."

A ruby ring, a gift from his father. He closed his eyes. He could see the ring on his mother's hand now. He'd always liked that glint of red.

He opened his eyes. Franny and the man were looking at him, waiting.

"Rubies, then."

Franny picked up a ruby tiara. "What is her hair like, Kit?"

"Thick. White."

"White-white or gray?"

"Snow-white. But not London snow. Pure-white country snow."

"Oh, then this would be perfect. The stones will look gorgeous against white hair."

"That's it, then."

"No, Kit, we should look at some other things."

"No," he said. "That's it."

"Do you think she'll love it?"

His mother would love a top from the toy shop if he gave it to her. He swallowed. "She'll love it."

The man nodded and turned away to place the tiara in a velvet-lined box.

"How about you, Franny? Should I get you a tiara?"

"Stop!" She giggled. "Tiaras are for married women or widows."

"How about a bracelet?"

"No." Her giggle fell away. "I really wouldn't enjoy any jewels."

"What would you enjoy?"

She tilted her head. "Can we go to a bookseller's?"

NATURALLY, she'd been to Hatchards before with her father. But it was an entirely different experience with Kit. The hush as he came in. The numerous deep bows. The large young man who immediately came from the back to carry His Grace's books for him.

"I'm their best customer," Kit said to her under his breath.

Of course, he was.

She'd been thinking about trying to snatch another kiss from Kit behind a shelf, but the young man doggedly followed behind them as Kit took her up a flight of stairs to the novels.

She knew what she wanted. She plucked three volumes from a shelf and handed them to Kit. "I want this." Then she snatched them back. "But I only want it if you promise to read it first."

"Yes."

She grinned. "Brilliant."

He took the books from her. "*Pride and Prejudice*. I've heard it's Prinny's favorite. Can't say I've used him as a judge of literary excellence in the past. Are you sure you don't want something else?"

"No. I love this book."

"Then you've already read it?"

"Of course." She swayed back and forth. "But I want you to read it. And then I want to talk to you about it. I think it could help you."

"But if you've already read it—"

"Lady LeClere's copy. I want my own."

"You don't want new boots instead?"

"Stop." She batted at him playfully with her reticule. "I want Elizabeth Bennet and Mr. Darcy."

"You fancy yourself a heroine in a novel? A—what was it?

—an Elizabeth Bennet?" He handed the three volumes to the young man.

"Oh, no. I'm nothing like her. I'm such a flibbertigibbet, and she's, oh, she's so wonderfully sensible."

If only she were an Elizabeth Bennet, but with a title. Then she'd be such a good match for—but she mustn't think that way. Wishes, horses, beggars.

Kit interrupted her foolish ruminating. "I've never come here and only bought one book. You must pick out more."

She considered. "I'll pick out one more."

"A dozen."

They settled on three. More and Lady LeClere might grow suspicious. She could never know about Franny staying alone with the duke and getting presents from him. Franny would be shown the door, and her plan to give Ren a wonderful Christmas would be for nought if that happened. He would have to leave school. They would both be consigned to the workhouse in the parish of Little Frittenden-Green.

But that wasn't going to happen.

It was going to be a Christmas Ren would always remember.

Just as Franny would always remember the Christmas kisses she had shared with the sweetest duke in all of England.

THIRTEEN

Only two more days until Christmas. Franny hugged herself in the hack. Better still, only one more day until Ren came!

They had gone shopping again today, and Franny held the parcel containing the yards of red ribbon Kit had bought for decorating. He'd also ordered a goose and potatoes and veg and oranges and chocolate and wine and ever-so many cakes and a Christmas pudding and all the greenery she wanted from Mr. Enys' stall. All those things would be delivered tomorrow.

But at the shops and stalls, Kit had teet-tottered on the edge of rudeness. He had been almost truculent. Something was bothering him. On the way to the next shop, he wouldn't look at her, didn't talk to her.

She wasn't helping him. She wasn't keeping her part of the bargain. And a silent, foul-tempered duke would cast a pall over Christmas.

"One step forward, five leagues backward," Franny ventured.

"Indeed."

Kit had clearly not heard what she had just said.

"Shall we practice kissing again?"

His head whipped around, and he looked at her for the first time in the last hour. She had gotten his attention. She smiled encouragingly.

But he glared back. "No."

Drabbit. She had hoped to use kissing lessons as an inducement for him, just as her own exasperated governess had used boiled sweets twenty years ago to get Franny to sit down and learn her letters. Franny knew next to nothing about teaching anyone anything, but she had always thought bribery was an excellent pedagogical method.

But she had really intended to reward herself, hadn't she? She wanted to kiss Kit again. And despite the peril, she was longing to tell him to give her an advanced kiss. A tupping kiss. A wedding night kiss.

He still glared at her.

Oh, the poor man.

"You don't like kissing me—"

"Absolutely untrue," he barked and looked away. "Or bosh, as you say."

She continued as if he had not interrupted her. "Because you're frustrated."

His neck went a dark red.

"I like you. You like me. You don't want to kiss me unless it's going to lead to more than a kiss."

"Yes!" It was a shout.

"And you've been so surly today. Is that the reason? Or have you finally discovered how really silly I am?" She tittered. "Or what a lot of trouble I am? Hauling you all over London? Forcing you to have a Christmas? Making you cook for me?"

"No," he mumbled. "I'm just an arsehole."

"I don't want you ever to say that about yourself again."

"It's true."

"No. It's not. It's your excuse, you darling man. Look at all the difficult things you get out of just by saying that." She made her voice into a gruff baritone. "I'm the Duke of Kittredge, and I'm an arsehole. So I don't have to go to Christmas house parties. So I don't have to be pleasant when I don't feel like it. So I don't have to—"

He winced. "Stop."

Oh, no, she had taken her jest too far.

"It's just I think you're splendid and everyone else should think so, too. Including you."

"Well, then we would all be as madly deluded as you are. Thank God, we're not."

No. This ended now.

"Fine. Let's have amorous congress."

KITTREDGE HELD COMPLETELY STILL. Was it possible she had said what he thought she had said?

She knocked on the ceiling of the hack, and the driver slid the little hatch open.

"Yes, Your Grace?"

She went forward onto her knees on the backward facing seat to talk to the man, giving Kittredge a superb opportunity to admire her bottom.

"Actually, Johnson, it's me." She had learned the hack driver's name, of course. "We're done shopping. Please take us back to His Grace's house."

"Yes, miss."

"There." She shut the little door and turned and sat. "Done. Because I promised myself I would never again bed an arsehole. *Ergo*, you're not one. And it should take care of your bad mood."

"Stop the hack," he roared.

She turned and slid the hatch open, but before she could utter a word, the driver said, "I heard, miss. Stopping now."

"Close that." Kittredge gestured. She closed the little door again and turned back to him, not the least bit affected by his shout. The hack rumbled to a halt.

He gritted his teeth before speaking. "Do not tease me."

"I'm not."

"You're sincere?"

"I am."

He got out of the hack but left the door open and went round to the front quickly, slipping in the melting, gray sludge.

The driver tried to stand up to bow. "Your Grace—"

"Sit," Kittredge snapped. He took a coin out of his purse and tossed it to the man who caught it, fumbling with the reins. "You can keep that sovereign if you can get us to my town house in five minutes without killing us or the horses."

"Yes, Your Grace."

The hack went like lightning, and yet it was still not enough haste for Kittredge. He opened the door to the town house and dragged Franny inside. He slammed the door and wrapped his arms around her and at last got his hands on her perfect arse.

God. Damn. So perfect.

"Kit." She laughed and pushed at him. "Let me take off my things."

He backed away, his cock already near bursting. He'd lost his hat somewhere, and he stripped off his greatcoat and tail-coat as Franny put her parcel and reticule down, removed her gloves, shrugged her way out of her pelisse, untied the bow on her bonnet, put the bonnet on a table, looked at her hair in the mirror—

"Enough," he growled and lunged forward and put his

shoulder to her stomach and grabbed around her thighs and headed up the stairs, her laughing all the way.

He got her on the bed and was about to take her, to plunge into her, to rut with—

And she told him to stop.

Christ almighty, she was the one who had suggested a fuck!

And then he saw her face. Anger, the beginning of tears. So like the look she had had when that villain had been touching her in the coach.

But today *he* was the villain.

Five leagues backward, indeed.

She hated him now like every other woman in the world. He sat on the edge of his bed and cursed himself, his cock, the animal who lived inside him.

A truth bubbled up, and he let it out. "I would like to please you."

"Why?"

He couldn't answer that.

"Do you want to please me because I'm your teacher? Or are you a selfish pig-widgeon and you think pleasing me will get you what you want?"

"I'm a selfish pig-widgeon. But I don't want to be." He gulped. "With you."

Her boots landed on the floor. She nestled next to him and touched his chest and laughed and he held her hand and somehow he knew everything would be all right between them.

And that rightness was more important than any so-called amorous congress.

He stared into her beautiful eyes. "Will you tell me what to do?"

"Of course, I will."

She laughed again, and he laughed with her. Because she

was laughing and she didn't hate him and because she still wanted him.

Laughing felt almost as good as her arse had in his hands.

"All right," she said, sitting up. "Let's have a chat first."

He looked up at her.

"As you know, I'm illegitimate. And while I adore my brother and don't think too badly of myself, I cannot bring another bastard into the world. So we have to make sure that doesn't happen."

His mind raced. "I could, I mean, we could not fuck— We could do other things." He had heard of men bringing women to climax with their hands or mouths. He, the selfish arseh— uh, pig-wigeon—had never done it himself, but Franny had promised to tell him what to do.

Was that a flicker of disappointment he saw on Franny's face?

An alternative. "Or, or, or I could spill outside of you. *Coitus interruptus.*"

"Yes," she said. "Or do you have a French letter, Kit?"

"No. But I could go buy one."

"Or two." She smiled. Did that mean what he thought it meant?

"Or three. Or a baker's dozen." He started to get up, but she laughed and put her hand on his chest again, and he relaxed back.

"Oh, Kit. I'm delighted you're so vigorous. But if you think you can control yourself, you can spill outside of me."

"I can control myself. I have a lot of practice controlling myself."

"I think you must. That fellow on the stage coach was lucky to escape without a thrashing, wasn't he?"

He wasn't about to tell her he had wanted to break the man's neck.

"Oh, one more thing?"

He nodded. At this moment, lying on his bed, talking with Franny, her so close, her hand on his chest, he felt no urgency. He knew the act with Franny was going to be revelatory and earth-shattering, but she had promised it would happen, and he believed her. There was no hurry.

She smiled wistfully. "When we talked about kissing, I wanted you to pretend you were kissing a belle of the *ton*."

No one but Franny had been in his mind for the last three days. "Yes."

"But I want you to make love to *me*. To Franny."

That's exactly what he wanted to do. He got up on his elbow and traced the pattern of the counterpane with his finger. "Why?"

"Oh, maybe I'm a little jealous of that virtuous, legitimate girl who's going to nab your heart."

He looked up to see if she was grinning. She wasn't.

"Besides I really don't want to imagine what other women want in bed from you. I know what I want."

"Which is?"

"I want everything." She opened her arms wide. "I want softness and tenderness to start. I want touch, I want skin. I want to see you. I want you to see me. And then a growing need and pressure, roughness, heat. I want the beast you just showed me. I want you to want me. I want to want you."

"There's no dearth of want on my end, Franny. Believe me."

Again the laugh. And she bent over and kissed him lightly on the lips. Suddenly his heart was as full as his cock had been just minutes ago.

You're beautiful, I cherish you, I adore you.
No.
I love you, you impossible woman.

Fourteen

She was dying to see him, touch him. She untied his cravat as he lay on the bed. He reached for her dress.

"If it's all right, Kit, I'll undress you first. Then you can do me."

"Oh."

"You might get too distracted by my beauty and forget to shed your trousers." She laughed, thinking of her unfashionable plumpness below the waist, but he nodded gravely.

"Very wise."

His cravat was off, and she brushed her fingertips over his neck. Even with no valet in the house, his skin was shaved smooth. She leaned over, and he quivered a little as she covered his throat with kisses. But he did not grab at her.

"You're being so good, Kit," she cooed against the pulse under his jaw. "This is the first bit, the soft part. It's pleasurable, isn't it?"

He didn't answer, but she felt his pulse quicken under her lips.

"Will you get off the bed for me?"

He stood, and she tried to ignore the sagging fall of his

trousers, the recrudescence of his tumescence. She unbuttoned his waistcoat and removed it. She slid his braces down his arms. All the while, he watched her with his hungry eyes.

Now the shirt. She reached and undid the top buttons and pushed the linen up, running her hands over his abdomen, the planes of his chest.

"I'm not tall enough. You must take it off."

He whipped his shirt over his head and she saw the beast again for a moment. But then he was still once more. Waiting as she had asked.

Her eyes traced the line of his shoulder that had carried her up the stairs. His arms showed the muscle she had felt every time he had held her. His hard manly chest with the smallest bit of brown hair in the center, going down, down, down… *not yet, Franny.*

She knelt at his feet, and he sucked in a breath.

"Sorry." She grinned. "Don't get too excited. I'm just taking off your shoes."

He laughed, all on his own. "I'm that transparent?"

She busied herself with the laces. "No. Your cock is."

Another solo laugh from her Kit. She joined in.

"I didn't know," he said.

"What?" She tapped his leg and he lifted it and she took off his shoe and reached up under his trouser leg to pull his stocking down.

"That laughing could be part of this."

"Only when it's good." She got the other shoe and stocking off and stood, brushing her hands together. "Back away a little." She sat on the bed. "Take off the trousers."

With no hesitation, he skimmed the brown wool down to his ankles and kicked the trousers off.

His legs were as muscled as his arms and with more brown hair like the hair on his chest and at the base of his cock.

Yes. His cock. It was fully upright. Girthful and tall.

Swollen with need. A drop glistened at the tip and all she'd done was kiss his neck and touch his chest. But the air in the room was thick with their mutual desire. She ached and pulsed and pressed her own thighs together.

"I'm the luckiest girl in the world today," she murmured. "You're so…so…"

He snorted. "Scrumptious?"

"Divine."

He shifted his weight back and forth. But there was no embarrassment or self-consciousness at her obvious ogling or her compliment about his form. But maybe some impatience?

She stood. "Go slow," she warned. "No ripping. This is my favorite dress, and I only own three."

"Yes. No ripping."

She turned, and he unbuttoned her dress as slowly as she had unbuttoned his waistcoat.

A pause. "Pull it up or push it down?"

"Up." She raised her arms. "My bumptious bottom interferes."

As he raised the dress over her head, she heard him whisper, "Your beautiful bottom."

Her sweet, darling Kit.

She thought of how she had just minutes ago prayed that some girl would love him since she couldn't, she shouldn't.

Why did I wish for that when I adore him so?

Because I want him to be happy. Kit deserves happiness and understanding. He should never be alone again. That's my Christmas wish.

Three dresses.

That was going to change immediately if he had anything to say about it.

He moved to lay the red dress over a chair, ensuring no part of it was creased.

And now he was living his fantasy from Franny's first day in his house. He was loosening the lace of her stays. And the sound she made when he drew them up over her head—not the moan he had imagined, but a contented sigh that went straight to his cock—was a thousand times more arousing because it was real.

It was Franny.

His member twitched, and he had to take a quick step back to keep from staining her petticoat with his tip.

But he didn't reach around her to cup her breasts through her chemise. He was undressing her as she had asked. Her arms were still up in the air, and he lifted her chemise. Oh, the exquisite, pale beauty of the skin of her back, her little winged shoulder blades, the delicate architecture of her spine.

She had kissed his neck earlier so he leaned forward and brushed his lips against her nape, smelling her hair, feeling its soft tickle on his nose.

"Oh, Kit," she sighed.

She turned around.

Her breasts were not the breasts of his dreams.

They were better.

Because they were hers.

She wasn't a girl. She was a woman. So her breasts hung a bit lower than he had imagined. And the red, jaunty nipples weren't red. They were dark pink with areolas a shade lighter. And those areolas were large, capping her breasts magnificently. As generous as the woman who possessed them.

"Do you want to touch me?" she asked, almost shyly.

"Yes. Of course."

"Go ahead."

He would exert control, delay that pleasure. "I have to finish undressing you first."

He untied the drawstring of her petticoat. He raised his brows.

She answered, "Down. That can go down."

He nodded and just as she had for him, he knelt. He loosened the drawstring and gently pulled the petticoat down. Her cunt was inches from his face. He could smell her musk. He froze.

"Stockings," she whispered.

He forced his eyes and hands to move, undo garters, roll down thick wool stockings. Her hands were busy doing something to her head—taking out hairpins?

She was as naked as he, her dark-brown hair falling in waves around her shoulders.

He stood. "Would you turn around for me?"

Her face flushed pink, and her hands fluttered. "I looked at you, so I suppose it's only fair."

"Do you not want me to look at your ar—bottom?"

"It doesn't match the rest of me."

"You're beautiful. And I'm sure it's beautiful. So it does match."

"I mean it's so big, but…" She turned, and he saw her arse in all its nude glory.

Yes. He was right. Of course, he was.

Her arse was beautiful.

Her cheeks were pert and round and meaty and perfect. She put the Callipygian Venus to shame. The Callipygian Venus was a wasted crone compared to Franny.

And he knew he wasn't supposed to win every argument, but he was going to win this one.

"Your buttocks are breathtakingly gorgeous," he said. "Your buttocks derange me. They drive me mad."

He heard a giggle. "You can't blame my buttocks for that."

He stepped up to her backside and pressed himself to her, his cock against her lower back. "You feel my derangement?"

She took in a shaky breath. "Is that your pet name for it?"

She turned around, brushing his torso with her breasts. He put his arms around her, gazed into her eyes, and brought her fully against him. Her arms wrapped around his neck.

As he kissed her, his hands went to her arse, and he squeezed. *You're beautiful, and your arse is beautiful.*

For the first time, he put his tongue in her mouth. A soft stroking. And she opened her lips and received him and played her own tongue along his, as he kneaded and petted and fondled her arse.

Her voice was husky when she said, "Shall we go to the bed?"

He drew down the counterpane, and they got into the bed together.

They lay on their sides, facing each other.

"Touch me," she whispered.

He touched and kissed her face, her neck, her shoulders. He even nuzzled into the little tufts of hair under her arms as she giggled and squirmed.

He kissed her mouth deeply again as he brought his hands to her breasts. She moaned a little, and he felt her nipples pucker under his rubbing thumbs.

Was he pleasing her? She was so much quieter than he had expected. He was used to a woman making all kinds of sounds before and during the act. Loud yelps. Shouted oaths. Screaming.

Her own hands were exploring him, touching his chest, his abdomen, his arms, his flanks and back. She squeezed his buttocks and murmured, "You're not too ill-equipped in this area, either."

He snorted, and she laughed.

He slid lower on the bed and began to kiss her chest. Only after he had gone over every inch of the skin of her breasts with his lips did he move to a nipple. He felt it stiffen under the caress of his tongue. He sucked a little. Her fingers sank into his shoulders, and her pelvis arched towards him. He then paid the same attention to the other nipple.

"Oh, Kit. That feels good."

"Good." But was it? He wanted her writhing in ecstasy. He came back up to her face.

"Tell me what to do, Franny."

"I want to touch your cock."

He gulped. She ran her fingers lightly over his shaft. Ah. Sweet agony. Then she grasped him more firmly and began to stroke him.

She lay onto her back and spread her legs a little. "You touch me, too, Kit."

"Stop." He didn't want to spend in her hand. And he needed to pay attention to her instructions. "You have to tell me what to do. To you."

She stopped stroking but kept her hand on him. "Have you never touched a quim before?"

"Of course, I have, I just…I'm not sure anyone was very interested in showing me…I'm not sure—"

"I'd be delighted to tell you what I like." She released his cock. "You'll make me spend, all right? And then we'll move on to the next thing. First, put your hand between my legs."

Her confidence helped him believe he could do this. He put his hand between her thighs, a good six inches from her cunt.

"Cup me." She sat up a little and reached for his hand and brought it up to her mound. "Feel me. Be gentle."

She was so warm here. Her dark maidenhair was not as soft as the hair on her head but softer than the coarse tangle around his throbbing cock. He ran his fingers over her outer lips, the crease at the tops of her thighs, and then dared to delve deeper and touch her wetness.

She mewed when he found her entrance. Tentatively, he

slid the tip of his middle finger into her channel. Then a little farther.

She put her hand over his and brought the heel of his palm down on the top of her maidenhair.

"Press and rub here while you do that."

He did what she asked, moving his finger in and out of her, watching her face flush red, her pupils grow. He felt more wetness now. He was doing that to her. She gripped his head and brought his face down to hers and kissed him.

This was the kind of kiss he had wanted to give her in the music room two days ago. Unrestrained, rough, clumsy. And now she was the one initiating it.

She was panting. "Kit, touch my button. Please."

Her button?

"I'm sorry, I'm sorry, I'm a terrible teacher. I need you to take your finger out of me and move it to the top of of my cleft."

His soaked finger slid out and up and came against a nub of hardness.

She yelped.

"Did I hurt you?"

"No, no, no, no, you didn't. Brush it gently. Up and down. Oh, Kit, that's marvelous. That's," she swallowed, "brilliant. You're doing so well. Oh, my God."

Her legs were restless, her knees coming up then straightening, heels sliding on the sheet.

"A little faster. A little more, just a little." She pulled him to her again and took his mouth.

He rubbed her hardness a little faster and added a little more pressure. She grew wilder underneath him.

"Oh, Kit, you, so sweet, you're doing so…I'm going to… you're making me…"

Her body was against his, and he could feel all of her

clench over and over and over again, and the whole time she looked into his eyes.

"Ohhh," she said, putting her hand over his to arrest the movement of his finger. "Ohhhh."

It was over. She had spent.

And she hadn't screamed once. He suspected his mistresses had acted in bed with him as much as they had on stage.

He felt a hand on his jaw.

"Kit."

Her eyes were hazed, her lips swollen.

"Oh, Kit. Thank you." She stretched out, her arms going above her head, her toes pointing. "Oh, thank you. That was devastating in the best way."

He bent his head and kissed a nipple.

"What would you like now, Your Grace?"

He raised his brows, and she giggled.

"Before that. Shall I use my mouth on you?"

He took her hand from above her head and guided it down to his cock. "You don't need to."

"Ooooh. You're so hard already."

He cleared his throat. "For you."

"My Christmas Eve-Eve present."

"Do you really want to…?"

She sat up, and her hand began moving over his length. "I've wanted to—oh, since we met."

He tried to scoff. "I looked like a vagabond."

"Oh, no, Kit. You were handsome and mysterious and savage. I wanted to climb onto your lap and ride you all the way to London."

He had gotten harder and harder, not just from her stroking, but from the image she had created of them fornicating in the coach.

"Please." It came out as a strangled entreaty.

She lay back. "Slowly, at first."

"Yes." He was eager to begin but not eager for the coupling to be over.

He knelt between her legs, and she drew her knees up. He could see the wetness and swelling and redness from her arousal. He put his weight on one hand and used the other to place the head of his cock at her entrance.

He pushed into her. She mewed just as she had when he had put his finger inside her.

He went in farther, and the sensation was sublime. Her walls clung to him, pushed against his cock, surrounded him with heat and pressure.

She had one hand in his hair, the other on his shoulder. She anchored him as he eased himself into her celestial cunt.

"I like this," she whispered. "You feel so big. You fill me so completely." A pause. "What's wrong?"

"I'm not all the way in."

A gleeful laugh, a wicked grin showing her gap. "Even better. Give me more."

He pushed. Now, he really was completely seated inside of her.

"Oh, Kit. You're…you're decadent."

He wiped at his forehead with the back of his hand. "Can I move?"

"Oh, oh, oh, yes, yes, yes. Please."

He withdrew slowly and pushed back in.

Oh, my God. She was looking at him with such relish. And her lips. He came down and kissed her as she strained upward and met him. *You're beautiful, your cunt, your arse, your breasts, all of you. I cherish your laugh. I adore that you tolerate me.*

You're the only woman for me.

Her arms came around him tightly. He moved in and out,

and her kisses were as fervent as he could wish, but still he thought he should be doing more.

"Tell me what to do, Franny."

"Do what feels good to you," she said and hesitated.

"Tell me."

Her hands slid down to his buttocks. "When you come into me, right at the end, tuck your tailbone in, towards me. And when you withdraw, flex a little. Stick your bottom out."

He tried, and the first time he withdrew, he went too far, and his shaft popped out of her quim with a wet noise.

Damn.

She didn't giggle, didn't frown, but breathed out the words, "I miss your cock already."

He fumbled but managed to reinsert himself.

"Ahhhhh," she said.

He stroked in and tilted his pelvis towards her and stroked out and tilted away.

"Does it feel good, Kit?"

It felt the same. But, at the same time, it also felt better because it clearly felt better to her.

"Very. Good."

He built his speed gradually. He'd never taken time like this inside a woman. There were new pleasures to be had from making love rather than fucking.

There was skin. Touching. Kissing. Looking at Franny.

Her breathing changed, became as heavy as his. She was pushing up against him every time he slid his body up hers, plunged his cock into her.

"Yes." She tossed her head from side to side. "Fuck me, Kit. Fuck me."

He pushed in harder.

"Give me," she gasped as her head curled up from the pillow and she fixed her enormous black pupils on him with an intensity that made his spine tingle. "Give me the beast.

Like when you carried me up the stairs and threw me on the bed. Fuck me like you wanted to then."

He hesitated. She hadn't liked that before. Was *she* trying to please *him*?

The next word came out on a deep, guttural groan. "Now."

He did his best. His bollocks were aching for release, so he let every primitive part of him give power to his thrusts.

A growl burned in his chest and rose up and out of him with his grunts.

You're beautiful. I adore fucking you. I fucking adore you. I fuck you. Mine.

And then her channel clenched, she clenched everywhere, her eyes opening wide.

"Oh."

That was all she said.

Five more brutal thrusts and he pulled out and stroked himself, staring into her eyes.

By God. God. Holy…Christmas.

He splattered everywhere.

Fuckity-fuck damn hell.

He closed his eyes but then forced them open. He had gotten his spend on her face. A gout on her cheek. A blob on her chin. A drop on her bottom lip.

"Will you tell me when it's all right for me to laugh?" Her tongue came out and swiped her lower lip.

He couldn't speak. He just shook his head. She sat up and pulled him to the mattress.

"Come down here next to your messy fizgig."

He lay on his side, bending his elbow and using the side of his arm for a pillow as he gazed up at her and attempted to slow his breathing. She took a corner of the sheet and wiped her cheek and chin, her breasts and belly.

"I'm sorry," he got out. "I ruined it."

"Oh, no." She smiled and curled herself up, facing him. "That was wonderful. That was the best— You were perfect."

"The best what?"

"You know."

He wanted her to say it. "No, I don't."

"It will go to your head. Fine. Amorous congress."

It did go to his head. It went there and fizzed like champagne. It also went to his cock, and he felt the fatigued organ beginning to revive.

"I'll be even better next time," he promised.

"I'm sure you will be. You're an excellent pupil. But look how I've mussed you."

Her fingers began to comb his hair. He grabbed her around the waist and pulled her into him and lay back. She put her head on his chest. He closed his eyes. Franny's hand grazed his belly, his chest. She began to hum.

Was that *fa-la-la-la-la*?

"I love you," he said.

The humming stopped.

A giggle. "You're supposed to say that in the heat of passion, Kit. Then I'll know you don't mean it."

"I do mean it."

Silence.

"Don't worry. I don't expect you to love me back. I just thought you should know…how lovable you are."

She moved, her breasts nudging at him, and he felt her lips brush against his. "You're very lovable, too."

He kept his eyes closed and just tightened his arms around her and kissed her deeply.

You're the only woman for me.

Twelve days of Christmas and it wasn't even Christmas Day yet. He had thirteen days to get her to fall in love with him. And he had a teacher right here to tell him how to do it.

FIFTEEN

He woke to an empty bed and sunlight and was immediately flooded with an irrational panic.

Stop.

Franny could have gone back to her own bed. She could have risen early. Taken Bevel for a walk. Tried to make coffee on her own.

He hastily dressed and made his way to the kitchen.

Dear Darling Duke of My Heart:

> *Kit, you have done wonderfully well with your lessons. In fact, you're done! Congratulations! Full marks!*
>
> *I'm sure you've realized this is a farewell note. I'm a horrible coward and couldn't tell you face-to-face because I know I would have cried!*
>
> *The truth is I love you, too. How brave you were to tell me that first! I know it's silly for two people to fall in love so quickly, but we did, didn't we?*
>
> *But I absolutely agree with your mother. You should be married. You will make a devoted husband. And, I think,*

with some more work on your temper, you could be an ideal
father. Look how well you've trained Bevel and how much
he loves you!

But more "lessons" from me will not advance your
pursuit of a wife. And my heart will break, so best I go
now! For both our sakes!

But maybe, every Christmastide, you'll spare a few
thoughts for the silly girl you once kissed under the
mistletoe in your carriage house?

I'm off to meet Ren's coach! I'm sorry about all the
trouble and expense. Maybe the shops will take the things
back?

He blinked through tears and looked at the items piled on
the kitchen table. A velvet bag holding a gold watch. Yards of
red ribbon. A stack of books. The bag of sweets Franny had
chosen for Ren. And the practical, thick, wool stockings she
had also picked out for her brother.

You're not to worry. I have managed everything so
far, and I will continue to do so! Brilliantly, I
might add!

Just promise me one thing—never think of yourself or
call yourself an arsehole again.

I would never fall in love with an arsehole.

Sincerely, with all my affection and admiration,

Franny

There was a rap on the kitchen door, and his heart leapt.
She had come back.

He flung the door open, and half-a-dozen lads stood there
carrying greenery, wine, a goose, hampers of food.

"Delivery!" chirped the first lad and came in. Kittredge

stood silently as the rest trooped in and placed their bundles all around the kitchen.

"Happy Christmas!" They removed their caps.

Oh.

He went into his pocket and took out his purse and gave each one a pound coin. The first lad looked at his hand and let out a whoop. "I can get my girl the bead necklace she wants!"

Then they all had to wish him a happy Christmas again when it was the worst fucking day of his life, and they all wanted to shake his hand, not knowing he was a duke, the owner of the house.

Finally, he closed the door on their cheery shouts in the mews. At least someone was happy this Christmas.

Some girl somewhere was going to get the bead necklace of her dreams while Franny got nothing.

"HE NEVER CAME HOME, YOUR GRACE," Dagenham's haggard manservant mumbled.

"Where was he going last night?"

"A Christmas ball here in town. Then the club, probably. He's sworn off gaming at the moment, and you know what that means."

Yes, compensatory drinking.

Kittredge turned and walked quickly away, tugging on Bevel's leash. A hack was not to be found today for love or money.

He marched into the club with Bevel—rules be damned—and discovered Dagenham in the reading room, sprawled over two chairs, asleep. He was wearing fancy dress with a garish red waistcoat.

"Wake up, Dagenham. I need you."

The viscount opened bleary eyes. "Yes. No need to shout."

"I didn't shout."

"You did," a nearby voice said. A rustle and a silver head appeared. It was Burchester. Other lumps around the reading room began stirring, and Kittredge realized all of Burchester's lot were here: Sir Matthew Elliot, Danforth, Pike, the hulking Longridge.

He turned back to Dagenham as the other men began to complain.

"I need to talk to you," Kittredge hissed.

"Talk."

"Not here."

"I can't move. Have some pity."

"Franny ran away. You have to help me find her. I…damn it, I love her, William."

He was sobbing and being put in a chair and Bevel was trying to lick his face and someone was shoving a whisky in his hand and he heard Dagenham saying *Lady Francesca* and *has a terrible tendre* and *never seen him like this.*

He pushed the whisky away. Dagenham's voice said, "Well, can't let this go to waste."

Pike's voice. "A chit you're looking for? I know all about finding women. Where do you think she went?"

Kittredge wiped at his eyes and nose. "I don't know. She isn't received by anyone in London."

"Do you think she might have found a cheap room? You can get them for next-to-nothing in the rookeries. I can go hunt around," Sir Matthew Elliot offered, running his hand through his blond hair which fell in place perfectly as he did so.

"She only has stage coach fare—" Kittredge gasped and stood. "Little Fucking-Green!"

"He's gone mad," observed Burchester.

"No!" Kittredge sputtered. "Little Fucking-Green!"

"I think he's naming a place," Danforth said. His wig was askew.

Kittredge whirled and pointed a finger at the baron. "Yes!"

Longridge coughed. "Little Frittenden-Green?"

"Yes! That's what I said. Lady LeClere's house is where she's gone. With Ren!"

"A pet bird?" asked Burchester.

"Her little brother!"

Dagenham clapped Kittredge on the shoulder. "Get your carriage and go after her."

"My carriage is at Merrifield."

Longridge closed his eyes. "Which is next to Little Frittenden-Green."

The group broke into a cacophony of suggestions until Captain Jack Pike said "Ahoy!" very loudly and took control.

"First, Sir Matthew will check the rookeries for a woman and a boy who meet the specifications. Second, Burchester will scare someone up around here to shave Kittredge, and Danforth will find some coffee. Third, Longridge has the longest stride, so he'll go to my house and tell them to get my carriage ready for you. Fourth, I'm going to saddle up my horse that's at Madame Flora's and ride out for the first three posts and alert them of your need for fresh horses."

"Thank you," Kittredge said weakly.

"Think nothing of it, Your Grace," Pike said, a boyish grin replacing his usual arrogant smirk. "I like to run a tight ship, and I'm always happy to help a duke. Might be one myself one day, and I'll need all the help I can get."

Kittredge turned to Dagenham. "And you'll come with me?"

"I wouldn't miss it for the world."

In Captain's Pike light but luxurious carriage drawn by a crack team of horses, Kittredge cursed the London Christmas Eve traffic.

"Calm down." Dagenham crossed his legs, narrowly

avoiding kicking Bevel, who was taking up the floor. "Tell me about her."

He did. He told Dagenham everything. Well, not everything. Not about yesterday evening. But Kittredge told him everything else.

"But I never bought her new boots."

"And it sounds like you never got a chance to discuss *Pride and Prejudice*."

"I didn't even get a chance to read the book."

Dagenham raised his brows. "You. Didn't get a chance. To read a book?"

"No."

Dagenham fumbled in his pockets and came up with a flask. "Well, you should have. It would give you some hints about how to get her back. It's a good love story. And cold, aloof, hard-to-understand heroes who offend everybody? Mr. Darcy hasn't got a patch on you."

"You've read it?"

"I have."

Kittredge leaned forward. "Tell it to me."

By the time the carriage arrived at Lady LeClere's house, thanks to Dagenham's prodigious memory, Kittredge and Bevel knew all about Miss Elizabeth Bennet and Mr. Fitzwilliam Darcy. But Kittredge thought it strangely unromantic that the heroine had fallen in love with the hero after seeing his house.

"No," Dagenham said. "It wasn't the house. It's a joke. The noble sacrifice Darcy makes is what clinches the deal. He gave money to Wickham, the man he hates, just to save her family and her sister's reputation. And he kept it secret. A great ploy."

"I am to do something noble and self-sacrificing but make sure she never knows about it?"

"Exactly."

The carriage rolled to a stop, and Kittredge tore up the steps of the house and pounded on the door.

A butler answered.

"Franny!"

Kittredge pushed past the butler with Bevel at his heels as Dagenham said, "Pardon us. Happy Christmas. That madman is the Duke of Kittredge, and I am the the Viscount Dagenham. We are calling."

"The family is at the Marquess of Merrifield's Christmas Eve ball, Your Grace, Lord Dagenham."

Kittredge seized a footman by the shoulders. "Where's Miss Cranwell's room?"

"Topmost floor, at the end, on the right." The footman tried to answer and bow at the same time.

Kittredge ran up flights of stairs and knocked on the door but was too impatient. "I'm coming in, Franny."

He opened the door just in time to see a thin ankle and a large foot disappearing under the bed. It wasn't Franny's ankle or foot.

He took a deep breath. "Ren? I'm a friend of your sister's. Don't be frightened."

Silence.

"I know you're under the bed."

He heard a sigh and a rolling sound, and a dark-brown head poked up on the other side of the bed. The boy stood. He was small and thin and looked younger than thirteen.

His eyes. They were Franny's eyes. But hostile.

"I'm Kit."

The boy bowed. "Your Grace."

Dagenham came into the room panting. "I'm…Dagenham. Don't…mind me." He collapsed into a chair.

"Where is your sister?" Kittredge demanded.

Ren folded his arms. "I'm not telling you." His eyes went to Bevel. "Is that Bevel?"

Bevel barked at his name.

"Don't be frightened, he won't hurt you."

"I'm not frightened. Of him or you."

"Good. So, Franny told you about Bevel? And me?"

"Yes."

"Did she tell you I'm in love with her?"

"She said you told her you were in love with her."

"Did she tell you she loved me?"

The boy bit his lip. So like Franny. And as honest as Franny. "Yes."

"Then why won't you tell me where she is?"

"She's had enough trouble."

"I'm not trouble."

Dagenham coughed into his hand.

Ren scowled. "You've already caused trouble. No one is to know I'm here, and you've left the door open."

Kittredge turned and saw a cluster of maids and footmen in the hallway.

"Scat!" he said and lunged for the door and closed it.

Ren's face was stone. "Too late. Now Franny will lose her place. We'll go to the workhouse."

Kittredge shook his head. "No, no, no. You won't. I'll make sure you won't."

"My sister won't take your money."

If only there was some way he could give Franny money without her knowing about it. The anonymous, noble, self-sacrifice thing. But there was no sum that would ever be a sacrifice. Not for Franny.

If only he could marry her.

"Why can't you?" Dagenham asked.

As sometimes happened when he was under duress, Kittredge must have unwittingly given voice to his thoughts.

"A duke can't marry a bastard." He turned to Ren. "Please, no offense intended."

The boy shrugged. "I had a loving father, and for the first day of my life, a loving mother. And an older sister who is like a mother to me. And who will do anything for me. And I'd do anything for her. A title can't compare to that. It's an unimportant distinction. Look at you, you're a duke." Ren wrinkled his nose. "One of the most powerful men in England, and you can't even marry someone you love. What's the point of being a duke if you can't do what you want?"

What's the point of being a duke if I can't do what I want?

There was no point.

From very far away, Kittredge heard Dagenham say, "Let His Grace stew, Cranwell. He'll come round in a moment. He's actually a fairly clever chap, just currently a bit unhinged by love."

"You're right," Kittredge said slowly. "There's no point whatsoever."

For the first time since he was a child, Kittredge saw a straight, shining road leading directly to a glorious future filled with light and love. Filled with Franny.

"Ren, I'm going to marry her."

"If she'll have you," Dagenham said warningly.

"Yes. If she'll have me. And if she won't have me, I'll…I'll slink away nobly and…work on the anonymous noble thing."

Ren looked to Dagenham who shook his head.

"Please tell me where she is," Kittredge begged Ren.

Dagenham said, "I'm sure the butler will tell us."

"I want my future brother to give me permission to marry his sister."

After a few long seconds, Ren sunk his hands into his pockets. "It's up to Franny. But you can't be worse than the other arsehole." He frowned. "That's where she is. At his house. What used to be our house. Lady LeClere's daughters said Franny must come to the Christmas Eve ball to sit with their mother and keep her happy and occupied."

Kittredge clapped the boy on the shoulder and grabbed his hand and shook it. "Thank you, Ren. Thank you. I promise, I promise I'll be a good husband to your sister and you will never have to worry about her again." He headed for the door.

But Dagenham didn't move and Bevel barked once, a warning.

Kittredge looked down at his clothes. Brown wool trousers. A plain waistcoat. No cravat.

"Shit," he said aloud before he could stop himself.

Ren pointed one hand at Kittredge and one at Dagenham and then crossed his arms. "Switch."

Sixteen

agenham's clothes were a tight fit, and Kittredge prayed for no split seams as he elbowed his way through the hellishly hot front hall.

It was far too noisy. How was he going to find Franny if he couldn't hear her laugh? Men's voices said his name, women gasped, music came from the ballroom, but where was that remarkable laugh?

Because Franny would be laughing at a ball, he just knew she would. She'd be delighted by the decorations, the gaiety, the company. She'd be wearing a red velvet dress and sipping wine. Or she'd be dancing with some smiling, flaxen-haired fool of a dandy who could tell amusing stories to make her laugh. Some piece-of-shit Bingley but with wit and more confidence. Some prickhead Wickham but with money.

He faltered. A Christmas Eve ball was where she belonged. Not sitting in a dark library with him. He was so damn selfish. What could she possibly want with him, the dismal Duke of Dourness? And he still hadn't come up with a noble sacrifice he might perform for her. An anonymous act of benevolence that would make him worthy of her.

He should leave.

No. No. He'd ask her. He had to. So she'd know her lessons had worked. Not only had he fallen in love, he'd found the woman he wanted to be his wife. She deserved to know. He'd let her decide.

He took a deep breath and plunged into the ballroom. He stood for a moment to look at the couples. No, thank God, she wasn't dancing with another man.

Then he saw her on the far side of the ballroom. She was seated, nodding her head. She wasn't laughing. She wasn't even smiling. And she was in the same red wool dress she'd been wearing last night.

Unacceptable. The not-laughing, the sitting on the side, the old dress were all entirely unacceptable.

She deserved to glow like the ruby she was. And if nothing else, he could be her setting, the thing that protected all of her beautiful, glittering facets.

And then she could shine, forever.

FRANNY NODDED when Lady LeClere said the ballroom was overly warm. She nodded when Lady LeClere said ballgowns had become far too revealing. She nodded when Lady LeClere said Franny wasn't dressed properly for a ball but at least she wasn't displaying her bosom like every other girl here.

Of course, Lady LeClere's daughters were tired of dancing attendance on their mother and were ready to dance themselves. And, see, Lady LeClere's youngest daughter was now partnered with her own husband. How romantic. How good it was Franny had come to the ball so Lady LeClere's daughters could enjoy themselves.

But if it was good, why did she feel like crying again? Surely, she had wept gallons in front of her poor brother today.

She must think of Ren. She'd see him after the ball. She'd wake him up when she got back to her room and tell him the good things. Like how Inchley, the butler, had gotten tears in his eyes when he had seen Franny. No, not that. And she wouldn't mention how she had hovered behind Lady Le-Clere's daughters in the receiving line and how Michael had said nothing, only sneered at her. She'd tell Ren instead about how pretty the ballroom looked. They'd never had a Christmas ball when their father had been the marquess.

A commotion stirred the other side of the ballroom, and Franny saw Kit stalking across the floor without a care for interrupting the figures of a country dance. His hair was wild, poking up everywhere, but he was in full dress. Black satin breeches, black tailcoat, intricate white cravat, but what was that? A red waistcoat. Twinkling. Covered in beads or spangles reflecting the candlelight of the chandeliers.

He was coming towards her, and she was unable to move. Even as Lady LeClere and the other women around her were getting to their feet and saying "Your Grace," and curtsying, she couldn't move.

He was directly in front of her. His eyes weren't hungry for once. They were as soft as his lips.

"Franny," he rasped and fell to his knees and buried his head in her lap and wrapped his arms around her waist.

Without thinking, she sank her fingers into his thick hair and stroked his head, trying to get the tufts to lay down the right way. Her darling, dear Kit, looking so grand. The reason for all her tears and now all her happiness.

"I missed you," he said into her lap just as she said the same thing.

He raised his head. She saw tears in his eyes.

"Did you really?"

"Yes, Kit."

"Oh, Franny." His hands pulled her head down. He was

kissing her wildly, frenziedly. Scrumptiously. And he was speaking as he was kissing, talking into her mouth, into her cheek, even into her nose.

"I love you, I love you, I love you, I love you. Marry me."

She got her mouth next to his ear. "Your Grace, you've just ruined me."

He pulled back and looked at her. "No, you've ruined me. You will marry me, won't you? Please, Franny. Please, Miss Francesca Cranwell?"

She shook her head. "I'm not legitimate."

"I don't care. I want to marry the woman I love. I want her always laughing. I want her to give everything we own away. I want her to be able to talk freely to everyone in the world without fear because I'll be next to her, protecting her from villains. I want to say *my wife* and have it be true."

"You could do so much better than me."

He scowled. "No. No one could be better than you. I'm sure you're right, and the other girls are perfectly nice, but I love you."

"You might love somebody else if you got to know her."

"I don't think so. And she wouldn't love me. But you do, don't you, Franny?"

"How could I not?"

"Very easily. Please just say yes, you love me."

"Yes, I love you, you wonderful nonsense man."

"Even though I haven't done some Darcyesque noble thing for you?"

"Darcyesque? You love me. That's noble." She leaned forward and whispered, "And you forgot. I've already seen your house. And your cock."

He laughed, the biggest laugh she'd ever heard from him. The music stopped as a hand appeared on Kit's shoulder. A thin, bony, aged hand with a ruby ring.

Kit looked up and scrambled to his feet. Franny followed

suit and when Kit bowed to a white-haired woman, Franny curtsied.

"Your Grace," Kit said.

"No, I'm Mother," the woman said and embraced him. "I couldn't be more overjoyed to see you, Ambrose. Happy Christmas. And a red waistcoat. How daring. What a treat."

"Mother, this is Franny. Miss Francesca Cranwell."

"Your Grace," Franny said and curtsied again.

"I lied," the Duchess of Kittredge said. "I *could* be more overjoyed. And I am. Delighted to meet you, Miss Cranwell. Of course, I knew your parents. Wonderful people, the most adoring couple. You have your mother's eyes." She turned her own pale-blue eyes to Kit. "And I saw you on your knees, Ambrose. Does that mean what I think it means?"

"I'm in love, and she said yes."

The duchess gasped. "Give her a ring before she changes her mind." She slipped something into her son's hand.

Kit looked at his hand and then looked at his mother. "But His Grace gave—"

"I remember your father here." She tapped her breastbone. "The ring should go to the next Duchess of Kittredge."

Kit kissed his mother on the cheek, and Franny saw tears come to the woman's eyes.

"Give your bride her Christmas present, dearest."

Kit turned to Franny and took her hand and slid the ring onto the smallest finger of her right hand. It fit perfectly.

The duchess embraced Franny. "Thank you, my dear. You're just what Ambrose needs."

"She's what I want." Kit took her hand.

"And I want you." The rest of the ballroom faded away as she stared into his eyes. Those stormy eyes that belied his steady, certain center.

A dog barked loudly, and someone screamed.

"Bevel!" Franny and Kit said at the same time.

Bevel trotted over to Franny. She rubbed his head. "Good boy. I'm sorry. The current marquess has an unaccountable fear of dogs."

Kit winked. "Shall I set Bevel on him?"

"Kit!"

"I'm joking."

"You can't fool me. You told me you have no sense of humor."

Kit started moving, keeping her close to his side. "I have a wonderful sense of humor. And *you* are the one who told me that."

"I never said *wonderful*."

"You win. You can always win. Now and forever. Ren and Dagenham are in the carriage. Where shall we go, Franny?"

"Home is where you are, Kit. Now and forever."

He stopped in the middle of the ballroom. "I know the archbishop. I could get a special license. There's no reason we couldn't be married by Twelfth Night."

Franny stared up at him. Twelfth Night?

"Kit?"

"Yes?"

"What's wrong with Christmas Day?"

FIRST EPILOGUE

Christmastide had been full to bursting with boughs of holly, games, music, outings.

And love.

Franny wafted love wherever she went.

His mother had come from Merrifield for the Christmas Day wedding and had spent five days afterwards with them in the servantless town house. When she had left, the now-dowager duchess declared she had laughed more in those five days than she had since his father's death.

The house was quiet. No servants had yet returned. Ren had gone back to school this morning in a private carriage.

Thirteen-year-old boys could be prickly. Especially where their sisters were concerned. But if Kittredge could one day make a friend of Ren, it would be an accomplishment. Not a noble act, but an accomplishment.

Bevel would help there. As would Franny.

Kittredge's wife sat cross-legged on the bed, a book on her lap held open with one hand and the other hand busy petting Bevel. She was wearing nothing but her spectacles and Kittredge's shirt, and he liked to see her that way. Of course, he'd rather see her naked, but Franny could wear whatever she liked.

Bare-chested, he carried a tray into the warm room and put it on a table. "Your Grace, dinner is goose."

Kit had burned the goose on Christmas Day and had cooked one every day since then.

She took off the spectacles with a charming *moue*. He loved every expression that crossed her face, and he hadn't seen this one before.

"I hate to be ungrateful when you've gone to all this trouble, but I'm tired of goose. The hungry families in Petticoat Lane who eat most of the goose the next day are tired of goose. Yesterday's goose was perfect. I have full faith you can cook a Christmas dinner."

"Good. We can go direct to our pudding."

Her eyes lit up. "Is it the same trifle as yesterday? The one with raspberry jam?"

"No. It's you."

She laughed her remarkable laugh as he bounced onto the bed next to her, making Bevel jump off and go in search of his own dinner.

Kittredge had one more Christmas present for Franny besides the boots, the dresses, the gloves, the three crates of novels he had gifted her over the last twelve days.

"Let's go to Italy for our wedding trip in a fortnight. Get away from the cold and the gray. Look up some of your mother's relations. I don't want to wait for a baby to make our family a little bigger."

"Oh, Kit!"

Now she was the one bouncing onto him, and his own laugh was smothered by her kisses.

"But if you're hungry, I'll make you some raw toast."

"I don't want dinner, Kit. I just want you. And Italy. But first, you."

He pulled his shirt off her as her hands slid over the trousers he had worn to the kitchen, frantically unbuttoning and tugging until she had him naked. Then she was atop him, and he had his hands on her as he liked, one on a breast, one spanning her bottom.

She was squirming, rubbing her sweet, wet quim over his cock as she kissed him with her tongue and teeth and her Franniness.

He moved his hands to her waist, desperate to be inside her and yet more desperate for something else.

"Come here."

He roughly grabbed and dragged, and she giggled until he got her upright, suspended above his face, her knees on either side of his head.

She looked down. "Kit?"

"Take hold of the headboard. The duke wants his dessert. Now."

Over the last twelve days, there had been trysts in linen closets, bathrooms, on sofas when his mother and Ren took Bevel for a walk, and in this bed during the long, winter nights. Franny had taken Kittredge into her mouth several times to his immense pleasure, but it had required some coaxing from him for her to let him do the same.

"He didn't like it," she had said. Kit knew *he* was the former Sir Michael Sempleton. "You might not like it, either."

"Let me find out."

And he had found out he *loved* it. To be right at the beating heart of Franny's excitement, to worship her, to taste her essence.

He hadn't made her spend the first time he tried using his tongue. But he had aroused her, and she had trembled and gone red and begged him to fuck her, and then she had climaxed very quickly with him inside her. The next night he had made her spend, gloriously, his tongue in her cunt, her thighs clenching around him, her hands in his hair.

But this was a new position.

He settled both his hands on her beautiful, plump, round bottom, holding her in place.

"I don't know if I can—"

"Please," he said and kissed what she called her button very lightly.

"Whatever His Grace—" he kissed her with a little more pressure, "—waa-ah-ants. Ahhhh, yes."

She was even more beautiful this way. Her sex above his face, her soft legs surrounding him, the undersides of her breasts visible and framing her face from his vantage.

He made his tongue into a point and holding her gaze, he stroked from her opening up to the top of her cleft.

She wobbled a bit. "Oh, my God."

"I've got you, Franny."

Then he devoted himself to feasting on her wetness, her tender flesh. She moaned quietly and writhed above him but kept her hold on the headboard, and he kept his hold on her bottom and his mouth on her sex.

"Kit, please, please, please."

He released one cheek of her bottom and reached up and pinched a nipple and made his tongue into a point again and licked and lashed at her little bit of hardness over and over again, faster and faster, harder and harder.

"Oh, oh, oh, oh."

She shook and Kittredge could hear the creak of the headboard as she pulled on it and she was very wet and swollen on his mouth and then she was crumpling and he was moving and sitting up as she slid down and he was holding her.

Her whole body was soft in his arms. No tension remained. She had completely surrendered to him. His luminous Franny.

His hard member was between them as he held her on his lap, her legs now around his waist. But his cock could wait. Franny would demand it soon enough with him either beneath her or on top of her or behind her where he could see and touch her arse while being inside her.

"You came," he said.

She pulled her head from his shoulder and looked at him. "Me and the Magi."

"You and the—? Oh, Twelfth Night. The last night of Christmas."

She kissed him. "Happy Christmas, Kit."

"No. Happiest Christmas ever. How shall we celebrate Epiphany tomorrow?" He dotted her face with kisses. "Games? An icy picnic on Hampstead Heath? Skating on the Serpentine? What does my duchess want?"

She closed her eyes and for the first time, she spoke her mother's tongue to him.

"*Un caminetto acceso, un libro, un cane…e tu.*"

He held still. This was another layer of his beautiful Franny. *My wife.*

She opened her eyes. "It translates to a fire, a book, a dog…and you."

"Yes," he breathed.

After a long, soft kiss, he toyed with her hair. "You must continue to be my teacher and tutor me in Italian before our trip."

"You need only one phrase, Kit. One. And it will make your life so wonderful and easy. *Mia moglie ha sempre ragione.*"

He repeated it back to her. "But what does it mean?"

Her serious face was starting to dissolve into a grin. "It means…" A giggle escaped. "It means my wife is always right!"

Kittredge didn't tickle Franny for too long. After all, there were so many other things to do when a man was in bed with a woman who inspired love, lust, and laughter.

All year round.

More

Duke the Halls has a second epilogue (a novelette about Kit and Franny's trip to Italy) that is only available to Felicity Niven's newsletter subscribers. In addition to getting this free second epilogue, subscribers to Felicity's newsletter receive dispatches from the writing trenches, news about upcoming romance releases, and other free stories. Subscribe at

www.felicityniven.com/dukethehalls

Duke the Halls is a Christmas story as well as the prequel novella to ***The Bed Me Books***, a series of steamy romances full of female sexual agency and happily-ever-after endings. Each novel begins with a woman making a seemingly simple request to a man: "Bed me." Of course, nothing is simple before, during, or after the bedding, and soon these gentlemen are in deep trouble, their hearts well and truly lost to the women in question. There is an excerpt from ***Bed Me, Duke***, the first novel in ***The Bed Me Books*** series in the pages ahead.

Author's Afterword

Franny became a neologist (someone who creates new words) because I was dying to use the word *scrumptious* in this story. But, of course, that word was not in the lexicon in 1817.

Finally, I thought, "Why couldn't Franny invent *scrumptious*?" Thus, a neologist was born.

It's important to know that these new words are intentional on her part and on mine. These are deliberate neologisms, not malapropisms.

And in case there is any question lingering in your mind, Kit is *not* an arsehole. He is neurodivergent and misunderstood by others as much as he misunderstands.

Obscuring Bevel's species for several chapters was inspired by the truly scrumptious ***Three Men in a Boat (To Say Nothing of the Dog)*** by Jerome K. Jerome.

The red spangled waistcoat Kit borrows from Dagenham was inspired by the brilliant (and brilliantly funny) ***When She Was Naughty*** by Tessa Dare.

Bed Me, Duke

Excerpt from Book 1 of The Bed Me Books

A desperate Scottish countess seeks lovemaking lessons from a gorgeous rogue.

He can't stand her fierce resistance to his charms. She can't stand his dazzling good looks. But why bother standing when they'd both prefer to lie down on a bed together? Especially since neither has any intention of falling in love.

Captain Jack Pike leads a blissfully carefree existence as London's richest and most notorious rake. Becoming the Duke of Dunmore would ruin his fun. He doesn't even know where Dunmore is—Scotland, maybe? To add insult to injury, the savage Countess of Kinmarloch refuses to swoon for him. But why should he care? Jack only beds women married to other men, after all, and there's not a man in the British Empire brave enough to wed the feral countess.

A countess in her own right, **Helen Boyd** must marry the new Duke of Dunmore to save the people of Kinmarloch from starvation. If only the troublesome Jack Pike would go away and stop torturing her with his handsome face, perfect male body, and shameless flirtation. On the other hand, Jack might be just the man to teach the woefully inexperienced Helen a thing or two about seducing the duke and luring him to the altar. And as part of her training, there would be the added advantage of bedding the most beautiful man she's ever seen.

Friction leads to fire leads to forever-after in **Bed Me, Duke**, the first book in the steamy Regency romance series **The Bed Me Books** from author Felicity Niven.

"Jack."

He held still, sure it was a dream.

"Jack Pike."

He sat bolt upright in the bed, heart pounding, a young lieutenant again, startled out of sleep by his commanding officer.

The Countess of Kinmarloch stood across the room, holding a candlestick.

"What's wrong, my lady?"

"Naething. Nae a thing. I didnae mean to frighten ye."

She hovered like a wraith in her nightdress while Jack was unclothed, not ready for battle stations. He clutched the blanket around his waist with one hand and reached out with other.

"Throw me my shirt, my lady. Behind you. On the chair."

Her burst of laughter fluttered the flame of the candle.

"Ye dinnae need to dress yerself for me, Jack Pike. I've seen yer chest. Ye were anxious enough to show it off to me a few days ago. I cannae believe yer shyness now."

Oh. Yes. Wake up, fool. Helen Boyd wasn't his superior officer. This wasn't a drill or a threat to the ship. He wasn't a youth, still in the navy. He was a man in his prime, naked in a bed. She was a woman who had confessed a degree of admiration for him and had come to his bedchamber in the middle of the night.

A woman in his bedchamber was a common enough occurrence in the life of Captain Jack Pike. He should be in complete command of the situation, himself, and the woman in question.

But it was *her*.

She took a step towards him. "And ye are clearly aware 'tis a handsome chest, ye vain man."

He made himself grin and lean back on the pillows, putting his arms behind his head, displaying himself and his handsome chest to her.

"I'm aware other females think highly of my chest, Helen, but I thought it might have escaped your notice."

She sat down on the edge of his bed, and her gaze dropped from his face to his torso.

She was looking at his muscles there, he thought. Or at the sprinkling of blond-brown hair that narrowed to a trail down to his navel and, lower still, to his cock, beginning to stir under the blanket.

Or perhaps she was looking at the scar under his left nipple, the scar he had sustained when he had been a little too intent on the chest of the lady on top of him and not on her foil-wielding husband who had come home earlier than expected.

Now Helen would ask him about the scar, and he would tell the lie he told all women, the lie about pirates that made most women stroke the scar before stroking something else on his body. Preferably something lower down.

But she didn't ask about the scar. And there was something in her expression he couldn't identify. It might be appreciation. It might be desire. Those sentiments were expected and welcome. But maybe…it might be…resentment?

No.

It was a trick of the candlelight.

Under the blanket, he began to respond more strongly to her presence, and he had to remind himself to keep his hands where they were, fingers laced together behind his head.

Easy, Jack. Don't spook her.

Because…Lady Kinmarloch in a nightdress, her hair in a plait. Lady Kinmarloch, smelling of cider and soap. Lady Kinmarloch, the one woman he might bed in the duchy of Dunmore without worry he was taking advantage since, after all, she was a countess. In her own right.

He had not had a woman in over a week, and a week was a very long time for Jack. He had thought he was going to have to wait until he returned to London, but with each passing second, it seemed more and more likely he would bed a woman much sooner than that.

Tonight, in fact. Here, in Dunmore Castle.

At the very least, her scent would feed his thoughts when he took himself in hand after she left his bedchamber. Even if he were mistaken about the reason she was sitting on his bed.

But he didn't think he was mistaken. She wanted something from him, and usually, there was only one thing women wanted from him, only one thing they knew they could get.

However, she was not a usual woman. Not by a long chalk.

She looked away. "Jack, naething which passes between us tonight can be spoken about, ever, to anyone. Including yer master."

She meant the Duke of Dunmore. Well, there was no difficulty there. He could assure her of that.

"My lady." His voice was a purr. "As I said this evening, I have no deep loyalty to the duke. We just know each other. As long as you don't lay a plot to assassinate the scoundrel, I promise you my complete discretion."

She whipped her head around and glared at him. "I mean it, Jack Pike."

He assumed his most serious countenance. "I won't tell anyone. You have my word, Helen."

He reached out to her lower back. She was all bone and muscle here, but there was warmth under the nightdress, and just a little lower down, her back began to curve out towards her bottom.

Her spine straightened under his hand, but she did not pull away. And was that a quiver? Promising.

She bit her lip before she spoke. "I have been thinking about the many beautiful ladies in London. And how the Duke of Dunmore could be easily persuaded to marry one of them." She swallowed. "But my land splits the duchy. If the duke and I were to wed, our son would eventually be both duke and earl and the divided lands would be one again."

Damn. He was wrong about why she was in his bedchamber.

But still. He did not remove his hand from her back. It felt so good right where it was. And Captain Jack Pike could easily steer the course of this encounter in an entirely different direc-tion. He could, and he would.

"Jack, do ye think that is enough?'

He blinked. "Enough for what?"

"For the duke to marry me."

"The duke might need to marry for money. It's nothing against you, Helen."

But I'd like to be against you. Very much.

She ducked her head. "Perhaps…I might have something else to offer?"

Oh, yes. This was even more promising.

He moved his hand along the top of her buttock, finding

the beginning of her crease, placing his fingertips there lightly. "What would that be?"

She met his eyes and took in a stuttering breath. "I know what I look like. But if ye would be willing to train me, I might be able to enrapture the duke. Get him to compromise me. Then he'd have to marry me."

Jack wouldn't have to steer anything at all. She was bearing right at him, under full sail. He bit back his gleeful grin.

"Train you?"

"Aye. Train me in the carnal arts."

"The what?"

She shook her head. "Ye know."

"I don't." This might be the most fun he had had in months. No, years. "What do the carnal arts consist of?"

Her voice had an edge to it. "What ye do with yer women, Jack Pike."

He sat up and leaned forward, his chest against her upper arm, and spoke in her ear. "Surely it's the same thing you do with your men."

"My men!" She shot up, almost clipping his chin with her shoulder. He caught her hand.

"Shhh, my lady. Sit back down. Give me that candle."

"My men," she muttered.

"Sit, Helen." He yanked her down so she was sitting on the edge of the bed again. She tried to pull her hand out of his grip, but he held her fast.

"I've changed my mind," she snapped. "Forget I said anything. Forget I was ever here. In fact, forget my name. I intend to forget yers as soon as I leave this room."

"Am I to understand you don't need my help?"

She stopped tugging.

"I wonder how far you'd get without me. You'll need some money to get to London. To buy some fine dresses. To get rooms. You'll need an introduction." He released her hand.

"Give me the money. I'll pay ye back," she hissed.

"How? How will you pay me back? You don't have a sixpence to rub together."

"I told ye my plan. I'm going to get the Duke of Dunmore to marry me."

"Oh, you think you can do that?" Jack laughed. "Without my help? Just a few minutes ago, you were in a bit of despair that you wouldn't be able to—what was the word?—*enrapture* the duke?"

She put her shoulders back and tossed her plait. This was the brave Helen he admired so much.

"Ye will train me, I will succeed, and I will be able to pay ye back."

"I am mystified as to why you think you need me." He shrugged. "I'm sure English love-making is not much different from Scottish love-making."

She scowled. Her large jaw jutted even more than it usually did, and he knew she was gritting her teeth.

"I. Have. Never. Been. Touched. By. A. Man."

He was rattled. "Er, that is to say, never? How old are you?"

"I am six and twenty."

Twenty-six and never touched by a man.

She tipped up her chin and looked at the ceiling. "I am the Countess of Kinmarloch, and before I was countess, I was in the direct line. Even if I were pretty, a lad widnae have dared touch me."

He shook his head. "Even if you were…Helen, look at me."

She turned her head and stared at him sullenly, her heavy brow suddenly heavier than ever.

"I know what I am. Dinnae pay me any of your compliments, Jack Pike. I dinnae need to hear them. And ye dinnae need to say them."

"Am I allowed to speak the truth, my lady?"

She snorted. "Ye widnae recognize the truth even if it had its fangs sunk into yer bollocks."

He winced. "Ouch. You have just conjured an extremely unpleasant image in my mind. Not at all conducive to putting me in the mood."

"In the mood?"

"First, to say something nice to you. Second, to train you."

Her eyes brightened. "Ye will agree then to train me?"

She was not at all interested in his flattery, his opinion of her looks, how he thought he could harvest her spare body for his own pleasure, and that her face…her face had grown on him, and in a certain light and at a certain angle, she looked almost attractive. No, she was only interested in what he could do for her. How he could further her ends.

"I was considering it seriously until you began to discuss fangs and bollocks."

The light in her eyes went out. "Ye feel I am too rough and coarse for a gentleman like the duke."

"Well, you could stand to have a little polish put on you, but I think a little roughness and coarseness is good."

She looked at him with suspicion. "I dinnae care what *ye* think, Jack Pike. I care what the duke thinks."

"The duke? Well…" He considered. "The duke likes a little coarseness and roughness. Just not mention of sharp things and genitals. Together, in the same sentence. Very off-putting."

"His Grace might nae mind me?"

"Mmmm." He licked his lips. "Not at all."

It was the truth. Because he, Jack Pike, didn't mind her. Not one bit. And the Duke of Dunmore's taste was the same as his.

Exactly the same.

Because he *was* the Duke of Dunmore.

Acknowledgments

Thank you to Alexandra Gall and Shannon Lawson, my generous friends who read this novella when it was not yet in its final form. And thank you to the lovely Gloria Pastorino who translated the Italian in the epilogue for me. However, all errors are mine and mine alone.

Finally, everlasting gratitude to my family—they are the ones who make Christmas magical.

ALSO BY FELICITY NIVEN

THE LOVELOCKS OF LONDON

When Ardor Blooms (prequel novella)*

Convergence of Desire (Book 1)

Clandestine Passion (Book 2)

A Perilous Flirtation (Book 3)

Harry's Christmas Present (short story)*

Love's Labor Lasts (novelette)**

THE BED ME BOOKS

Duke the Halls (prequel novella)

Bed Me, Duke (Book 1)

Bed Me, Baron (Book 2)

Bed Me, Earl (Book 3)

Jack & Helen & Phin & Caro (short story)*

Be Not Coy (short story)

Voluptuous (novella)

*available to newsletter subscribers

** part of *The Lovelocks of London: The Collection*

ABOUT THE AUTHOR

Felicity Niven is a hopeful romantic. Writing Regency romance is her third career after two degrees from Harvard. And you know what they say about third things? Yep, it's a charm. She splits her time between the temperate South in the winter and the cool Great Lakes in the summer and thinks there can be no greater comforts than a pot of soup on the stove, a set of clean sheets on the bed, and a Jimmy Stewart film on a screen in the living room. She is the author of ***The Bed Me Books*** and ***The Lovelocks of London*** series.

www.ingramcontent.com/pod-product-compliance
Lightning Source LLC
Chambersburg PA
CBHW021552310726
48972CB00003B/796